MOOMINPAPPA
AT SEA

TOVE JANSSON was born in Helsingfors, Finland, and grew up in a household full of books. She became a painter as an adult and studied art in Finland, Sweden, and France. She began writing for children as play, something apart from her serious work, and still creates children's books out of an enjoyment of fantasy. Ms. Jansson was awarded the Hans Christian Andersen International Medal for her Moomin books.

MOOMINPAPPA AT SEA

Written and Illustrated by
TOVE JANSSON

Translated by KINGSLEY HART

A CAMELOT BOOK/PUBLISHED BY AVON BOOKS

First published in English 1966.
Second (corrected) Impression (U.S.) 1968.

AVON BOOKS
A division of
The Hearst Corporation
959 Eighth Avenue
New York, New York 10019

First Camelot Printing, August, 1977

CAMELOT TRADEMARK REG. U.S. PAT. OFF. AND IN
OTHER COUNTRIES, MARCA REGISTRADA, HECHO EN
U.S.A.

Printed in the U.S.A.

The Log Book

To some father

THE ISLAND
LAT. 60° 7′ 12″ N.
LONG. 25° 45′ 50″ E.

THE GULF OF FINLAND

The Family in the Crystal Ball

One afternoon at the end of August, Moominpappa was walking about in his garden feeling at a loss. He had no idea what to do with himself, because it seemed everything there was to be done had already been done or was being done by somebody else.

Moominpappa aimlessly pottered about in his garden, his tail dragging along the ground behind him in a melancholy way. Here, down in the valley, the heat was scorching; everything was still and silent, and not a little dusty. It was the month when there could be great forest fires, the month for taking great care.

He had warned the family. Time and time again he had explained how necessary it was to be careful in August. He had described the burning valley, the roar of the flames, the white-hot tree trunks, and the fire creeping along the ground underneath the moss. Blinding columns of flame flung upwards against the night sky! Waves of fire, rushing down the sides of the valley and on towards the sea. . . .

"Sizzling, they throw themselves into the sea," finished Moominpappa with gloomy satisfaction. "Everything is black, everything has been burned up. A tremendous responsibility rests on the smallest creature who can lay his paws on matches."

The family stopped what they were doing and said: "Yes. Of course. Yes, yes." Then they took no more notice of him, and got on with what they were doing.

They were always doing something. Quietly, without interruption, and with great concentration, they carried on with the hundred-and-one small things that made up their world. It was a world that was very private, and self-contained, and to which nothing could be added. Like a map where everything has been discovered, everywhere inhabited, and where there are no bare patches left any longer. And they said to each other: "He always talks about forest fires in August."

Moominpappa climbed up the veranda steps. His paws got stuck in the varnish as usual, making little sucking sounds all the way up and across the floor, right up to the wicker chair. His tail got stuck, too; it felt as though someone was pulling it.

Moominpappa sat down and shut his eyes. "That floor ought to be revarnished," he thought. "The heat makes it like that, of course. But a good varnish shouldn't start melting just because it's hot. Perhaps I used the wrong sort of varnish. It's an awful long time since I built the veranda, and it's high time it was revarnished. But first it'll have to be rubbed with sandpaper, a rotten job that no one will thank me for doing. But there's something special about a new white floor, painted with a thick brush and shiny varnish. The family will have to use the back door and keep out of the way while I'm doing it. And then I'll let them come in, saying: 'There you are! Look, your new veranda!' . . . It's much too hot. I'd love to be out sailing. Sailing right out to sea, as far as I can go . . ."

Moominpappa felt a sleepy feeling in his paws. He shook himself and lit his pipe. The match went on burning in the ash-tray, and he watched it, fascinated. Just before it went out he tore up some bits of newspaper and put them on the flame. It was a pretty little fire, hardly visible in the sunshine, but it was burning nicely. He watched it carefully.

"It's going out again," said Little My. "Put some more on!" She was sitting in the shade on the veranda railings.

"Oh, it's you!" said Moominpappa, and he shook the ash-tray until the fire went out. "I'm just watching the way fire burns. It's very important."

Little My laughed, and went on looking at him. Then he pulled his hat down over his eyes and took refuge in sleep.

*   *   *

"Pappa," said Moomintroll. "Wake up! We've just put out a forest fire!"

Both Moominpappa's paws were stuck firmly to the floor. He wrenched them loose with a strong feeling of reluctance. It wasn't fair. "What are you talking about?" he said.

"A real little forest fire," Moomintroll told him. "Just behind the tobacco-patch. The moss was on fire, and Mamma says that it might have been a spark from the chimney . . ."

Moominpappa leaped into the air and in a flash became a determined man-of-action. His hat rolled down the steps.

"We put it out!" Moomintroll shouted. "We put it out straightaway. There's nothing for you to worry about!"

Moominpappa stopped dead. He was feeling very angry. "Have you put it out without me?" he said. "Why didn't anybody tell me? You just let me go on sleeping without saying anything!"

"But, dearest," said Moominmamma leaning out of the

kitchen window, "we didn't think it was really necessary to wake you up. It was a very small fire, and it was only smoking a little. I happened to be going by with some buckets of water, so all I had to do was to sprinkle a few drops on it in passing . . ."

"In passing," cried Moominpappa. "Just sprinkle. Sprinkle, indeed! What a word! And leaving the fire to burn under the moss unguarded! Where is it? Where is it?"

Moominmamma left what she was doing and led the way to the tobacco-patch. Moomintroll stayed on the veranda gazing after them. The black spot in the moss was a very small spot indeed.

"Don't imagine," said Moominpappa at last, very slowly, "that a spot like this isn't dangerous. Far from it. It can go on burning *under* the moss, you see. In the ground. Hours and perhaps even days may go by, and then suddenly, whoof! The fire breaks out somewhere quite different. Do you see what I mean?"

"Yes, dearest," answered Moominmamma.

"So I'm going to stay here," Moominpappa went on, sulkily digging in the moss. "I shall stand guard over it. I'll stay here all night if necessary."

"Do you really think," Moominmamma began. Then she just said, "Yes. That's very good of you. One never knows what will happen with moss."

Moominpappa sat all the afternoon watching the little black spot, first pulling up the moss for quite a way round it. He wouldn't leave it to go indoors for his dinner. He really wanted the others to think he was offended.

"Do you think he'll stay out there all night?" asked Moomintroll.

"It's quite possible," said Moominmamma.

"If you're sore, you're sore," observed Little My, peeling

her potatoes with her teeth. "You have to be angry sometimes. Every little creep has a right to be angry. But Pappa's
angry in the wrong way. He's not letting it out, just shutting
it up inside him."

"My dear child," said Moominmamma, "Pappa knows
what he's doing."

"I don't think he does," said Little My simply. "He
doesn't know at all. Do you know?"

"Not really," Moominmamma had to admit.

*   *   *

Moominpappa dug his nose in the moss and was aware of
the sour smell of smoke. The ground wasn't even warm any
longer. He emptied his pipe into the hole and blew on the
sparks. They glowed for a moment or two and then went
out. He stamped on the fatal spot and then walked slowly
down the garden to have a look in his crystal ball.

Dusk was rising from the ground, as it usually did, gather-
ing in under the trees. Round the crystal ball there was a
little more light. There it stood, reflecting the whole garden,
looking very beautiful on its coral pedestal. It was Moominpappa's very own crystal ball, his own magic ball of shining
blue glass, the centre of the garden, of the valley, and of the
whole world.

But Moominpappa didn't look into it straightaway. First
he looked at his grimy paws, trying to collect all his vague,
scattered and troubled thoughts. When he was feeling as sad
as he possibly could, he looked into the crystal ball for consolation. Every evening of that long, warm, beautiful and
melancholy summer he had done the same thing.

The crystal ball was always cool. Its blue was deeper and
clearer than the blue of the sea itself, and it changed the
colour of the whole world so that it became cool and remote

and strange. At the centre of this glass world he saw himself, his own big nose, and around him he saw the reflection of a transformed, dreamlike landscape. The blue ground was deep, deep down inside, and there where he couldn't reach Moominpappa began to search for his family. He only had to wait a while and they always came. They were always reflected in the crystal ball.

It was only natural, because they had so much to do at dusk. They were always doing something. Sooner or later, Moominmamma would bustle over from the kitchen side of the house towards the outside cellar to fetch some sausages or some butter. Or to the potato-patch. Or to get some wood. Every time she did it, she looked as though she was walking down a completely strange and exciting path. But you could never be sure. She might just as well be out on some secret errand of her own which she thought was fun, or playing some private game, or just walking round for the sake of it.

There she came, scampering along like a busy white ball, farthest away among the bluest of blue shadows. And there was Moomintroll, aloof, and keeping himself to himself. And there was Little My, slinking up the slope more like a movement than anything else, you could see so little of her. She was just a glimpse of something determined and independent—something so independent that it had no need to show itself. But their reflections made them all seem incredibly small, and the crystal ball made all their movements seem forlorn and aimless.

Moominpappa liked this. It was his evening game. It made him feel that they all needed protection, that they were at the bottom of a deep sea that only he knew about.

It was almost dark now. Suddenly something different happened in the crystal ball: a light appeared. Moominmamma had lit a lamp on the veranda, something she hadn't done all the summer. It was the oil lamp. All of a sudden the feeling of safety was concentrated on a single point, on the veranda and nowhere else; and on the veranda Moominmamma was sitting, waiting for her family to come home so that she could give them all their evening tea.

The crystal ball became dim and the blue all turned to black; the lamp was the only thing that could be seen.

Moominpappa stood there for a while without really knowing what he was thinking about, and then turned and walked towards the house.

* * *

"Well," said Moominpappa, "now I think we can sleep in peace. The danger should be over. But just to make sure, I'll go and check once more at dawn."

"Huh!" said Little My.

"Pappa," cried Moomintroll, "haven't you noticed anything? We've got a lamp!"

"Yes, I thought it was about time we started having a lamp now that the evenings are drawing-in. At least I felt so this evening," said Moominmamma.

Moominpappa said: "You've put an end to the summer. No lamps should be lit until summer is really over."

"Well, it'll have to be autumn then," said Moominmamma in her quiet way.

The lamp sizzled as it burned. It made everything seem close and safe, a little family circle they all knew and trusted. Outside this circle lay everything that was strange and frightening, and the darkness seemed to reach higher and higher and further and further away, right to the end of the world.

"In some families it's the father who decides when it's time to light the lamp," muttered Moominpappa into his tea.

Moomintroll had arranged his sandwiches in a row in front of him in the usual way: the cheese sandwich first, then two with sausage meat, one with cold potato and sardines, and last of all one with marmalade on it. He was completely happy. Little My was eating only sardines because she had a feeling that it was somehow an unusual evening. She gazed thoughtfully out into the dark of the garden, and her eyes became blacker and blacker the more she thought, and the more she ate.

The light from the lamp shone on the grass and on the lilac bush. But where it crept in among the shadows, where the Groke sat all on her own, it was much weaker.

The Groke had been sitting for so long on the same spot that the ground had frozen beneath her. When she stood up and shuffled a little nearer the light, the grass crackled like splintering glass. A whisper of fright rustled through the leaves, and a few curled up and fell with a shudder from a maple tree on to her shoulders. The asters leaned over as far as they could to get out of her way, and the grasshoppers were silent.

"Why aren't you eating?" asked Moominmamma.

"I don't know," said Moomintroll. "Have we any Venetian blinds?"

"They're in the attic. We shan't need them until we hibernate for the winter," Moominmamma turned to Moominpappa and said: "Wouldn't you like to do some work on your model lighthouse for a while, now that the lamp is lit?"

"Huh!" said Moominpappa. "It's too childish. It isn't real."

★   ★   ★

The Groke shuffled a little nearer. She stared at the lamp and softly shook her big, clumsy head. A freezing white mist hung round her feet as she started to glide towards the light, an enormous, lonely grey shadow. The windows rattled a little as if there were distant thunder, and the whole garden seemed to be holding its breath. The Groke came close to the veranda and stood quite still just outside the circle of light that shone on the darkened ground.

Then she took a quick stride up to the window and the lamplight fell right on her face.

Inside, the quiet room was suddenly filled with screams and panic-stricken movement, chairs fell over and someone carried the lamp away. In a few seconds the veranda lay in darkness. Everyone had rushed inside the house, right inside where it was safe, and hidden themselves, and their lamp.

The Groke stood still for a while, breathing frost on the window-pane of the deserted room. As she slid away she merged into the darkness; the grass crackled and snapped under her feet as she passed, and slowly she moved farther and farther away. With a shudder the garden dropped its leaves, and then breathed again: the Groke's passed.

*   *   *

"But it's quite unnecessary to barricade ourselves in and stay awake all night," said Moominmamma. "She's probably ruined something out there in the garden again, but she isn't dangerous. You know she isn't, even though she may be frightful."

"Of course she's dangerous," Moominpappa shouted. "Even you were frightened. You were terribly frightened actually—but you needn't be as long as I am in the house."

"But Pappa, dear," said Moominmamma, "we're afraid of the Groke because she's just cold all over. And because she doesn't like anybody. But she's never done any harm. Well, I think it's time we all went to bed."

"All right!" said Moominpappa, putting the poker back in its corner. "All right. If she's not the slightest bit dangerous, you won't want me to look after you then. That's just fine by me!" And with that parting shot, he went on to the veranda, grabbing some cheese and a sausage in passing, and stamped off into the darkness alone.

"Well," said Little My, impressed. "Good! He's blowing off steam. He'll go and stand guard over that moss till early in the morning."

Moominmamma said nothing. She padded up and down,

getting ready for the night. As usual, she looked in her hand-bag, she turned the lamp down; and all the time there was a silence in the room that didn't seem natural. When she came to Moominpappa's model lighthouse, standing on the shelf by the washstand in the corner, she began to dust it absent-mindedly.

"Mamma," said Moomintroll.

But Moominmamma wasn't listening. She went up to the big map hanging on the wall, the one showing Moomin-valley with the coast and its islands. She climbed on to a chair so that she could reach right out to sea, and put her nose right on a spot in the middle of nowhere.

"There it is," she murmured. "That's where we're going to live and lead a wonderful life, full of troubles . . ."

"What did you say?" asked Moomintroll.

"That's where we're going to live," repeated Moomin-mamma. "That's Pappa's island. Pappa is going to look after us there. We're going to move there and live there all our lives, and start everything afresh, right from the beginning."

"I've always thought that spot was only a bit of fly-dirt," said Little My.

Moominmamma climbed down to the floor. "It takes a long time sometimes," she said. "It can take a terrible long time before things sort themselves out."

Then she went out into the garden.

"I'm not saying anything about some mothers and fathers," drawled Little My. "If I do, the first thing you'll say is that they are never silly. They're up to something, those two. I'd eat a bushel of sand if I knew what it was."

"You're not supposed to know," said Moomintroll sharply. "They know perfectly well why they're behaving a little oddly. *Some* people think they're so superior and have to know everything just because they've been adopted!"

"You're dead right," said Little My. "Of course I'm superior!"

Moomintroll stared at the spot on the map, far out in the open sea all on its own, and thought: "Pappa wants to live there. That's where he wants to go. They're serious about it. This is a serious game." And suddenly he saw the sea round the island begin to rise and fall. The island itself was green with red cliffs. It was the island he had seen in picture-books, a desert island, inhabited by pirates. He felt a lump in his throat. "Little My," he whispered, "it's fantastic!"

"You don't say!" said Little My. "Everything's fantastic—more or less. The most fantastic thing about it all would be if we were to make a great hullabaloo about getting us and all our paraphernalia there, only to discover that it really was only a bit of fly-dirt!"

*   *   *

It could scarcely have been more than half-past five in the morning when Moomintroll was following the Groke's tracks through the garden. The ground had thawed again, but he could still see the places where she had sat. The grass there had turned quite brown. He knew that if she sat on the same spot for more than an hour, nothing would ever grow there again. The ground just died of fright. There were several spots like that in the garden, and the worst one, infuriatingly enough, was in the middle of the tulip-bed.

A wide path of dry leaves led all the way up to the veranda. That's where she had stood. She had remained outside the circle of light and stared at the lamp. She couldn't help it, she had to come as close as possible, and everything died. It was always the same. Everything she touched just died.

Moomintroll imagined he was the Groke. He shuffled along slowly, all hunched up, through a pile of dead leaves. He stood still, waiting while he spread the mist round him. He sighed and stared longingly towards the window. He was the loneliest creature in the whole world.

But without the lamp it wasn't very convincing. Instead, only nice thoughts came into his head, thoughts of islands in the sea, and great changes taking place in all their lives. He forgot the Groke and started to play a game as he walked between the long shadows cast by the morning sun. You had to walk only where the sun was shining. The shadows were the unfathomable depths of the sea. That is, of course, if one couldn't swim.

Somebody was whistling in the woodshed. Moomintroll looked inside. Bright gold sunlight shone on a pile of wood-shavings by the window, and there was a smell of linseed-oil and resin. Moominpappa was busy putting a little oak door in the wall of his lighthouse.

"Look at these iron clamps," he said. "They're buried in the rock, and this is how you climb up to the lighthouse. You have to be very careful if the weather's rough. Your

boat is carried in towards the rock on the crest of a wave—
then you jump off, get a firm grip and scramble up while the
boat is flung back . . . when the next wave comes, you're safe.
Then you fight your way against the wind, holding on to this
railing. Then you open the door, but it's heavy. Now it
slams behind you. You're inside the lighthouse. You can hear
the roar of the sea in the distance through the thick walls.
Outside it's roaring all round, and the boat is already a long
way off."

"Are we inside, too?" asked Moomintroll.

"Of course," said Moominpappa. "You're up here in the
tower. Look, every window has real glass. Right at the top is
the light itself, and it's red and green and white, and it
flashes at regular intervals all night, so that boats know
where to go."

"Are you going to put a real light in it?" asked Moomintroll. "Perhaps you could put a battery underneath and
somehow make it flash."

"Of course I could," said Moominpappa, cutting some
little steps to put in front of the lighthouse door. "But I
haven't time just now. This is only a toy, actually, just a way
of trying things out." Moominpappa laughed, a little embarrassed, and began poking about in his tool drawer.

"Wonderful!" said Moomintroll. "So long."

"So long," said Moominpappa.

The shadows were now much shorter. A new day was
beginning, just as warm and just as beautiful. Moominmamma was sitting on the steps doing nothing at all, which
seemed very strange somehow.

"Everybody's up so early this morning," said Moomintroll. He sat beside her, screwing his eyes up in the sun.

"Did you know that there's a lighthouse on Pappa's
island?" he said.

"Of course I did," Moominmamma answered. "He's been talking about it all summer. That's where we're going to live."

There was so much to talk about that nothing was said. It was warm sitting there on the steps. Everything seemed to be so right. Moominpappa began to whistle "Anchor's Aweigh", something he did rather well.

"I'll make some coffee soon. I just thought I'd sit here and think. It's been quite a night."

But the lighthouse was calling to them. They knew that they must go to the island, and go soon.

The Lighthouse

On the all-important evening of their departure, the wind had moved towards the east; it had got up soon after twelve, but they had decided not to leave before sunset. The sea was warm and deep blue, just as blue as it was in the crystal ball. The jetty was piled high with luggage, right up to the bathing-house, where the boat was lying tied-up. It was bobbing up and down, with its sail hoisted and a hurricane lamp was burning at the top of the mast. On the beach it was already getting dark.

*   *   *

"Of course we run the risk of it being calm tonight," said Moominpappa. "We could have left immediately after lunch. But on an occasion like this we must wait for sunset. Setting out in the right way is just as important as the opening lines in a book: they determine everything." He sat in the sand next to Moominmamma. "Look at the boat," he said. "Look at the *Adventure*. A boat by night is a wonderful sight. This is the way to start a new life, with a hurricane lamp shining at the top of the mast, and the coast-line disappearing behind one as the whole world lies sleeping. Making a journey by night is more wonderful than anything in the world."

"Yes, you're right," replied Moominmamma. "One makes a trip by day, but by night one sets out on a journey." She was rather tired after all the packing, and a little worried in case something important had been forgotten. The pile of luggage looked enormous now that it was all there on the jetty, but she knew how little it would seem when they unpacked. A whole family needs such an awful lot of things in order to live through a single day in the proper way.

But now, of course, things were different. Now the proper thing to do was that they should begin an entirely new life, and that Moominpappa should provide everything they needed, look after them and protect them. Life must have been too easy for them up till now. "It's strange," Moominmamma thought. "Strange that people can be sad, and even angry because life is too easy. But that's the way it is, I suppose. The only thing to do is to start life afresh."

"Don't you think it's dark enough now?" she said. "Your hurricane lamp looks really lovely against the sky. Perhaps we might start now."

"Just a moment, I must get my bearings," said Moominpappa. He spread out the map on the sand and stared at the island, all by itself right out in the open sea. He was very serious. He sniffed in the wind for a while and tried to get his sense of direction, something he hadn't had to use for a long time. Our ancestors never needed to worry about finding the right course, it came to them naturally of its own accord. It's a pity that the instinct gets weaker if you don't use it.

After a while, Moominpappa felt that he was sure he had
the right course. He knew which way to go, so they could set
sail. He put his hat straight and said: "Let's be off. But
you're not to lift a thing. We'll do all the heavy work. Just go
aboard."

Moominmamma nodded, and somewhat wearily dragged
herself to her feet. The sea had turned violet and the line of
the forest along the shore looked soft and dark. She was very
sleepy, and suddenly felt everything was a little unreal; a
slow, fantastically lit dream in which one walks through
heavy, heavy sand without getting anywhere.

The others were on the jetty, putting the luggage on
board. The storm lantern swayed to and fro, and the
silhouette of the jetty and the bathing-house looked like a
long spiky dragon against the evening sky. She could hear
Little My laughing, and behind her the cries of night-birds
still awake in the forest.

"It's so beautiful!" said Moominmamma to herself.
"Beautiful and just a little strange. Now I've time to think
about it, the whole thing *is* rather wonderful. But I wonder
whether Pappa will mind if I take a little nap in the boat."

*   *   *

The Groke slunk through the garden after sunset, but this
evening there was no lamp on the veranda. The curtains
had been taken down and the water-butt had been turned
upside down. The key hung on its nail above the door.

She was used to deserted houses, and she saw at once that
no one would light a lamp here for a long time to come. She
shuffled slowly back up the slope towards the cliff. For a
moment the crystal ball caught her reflection, but then once
more was filled with its usual, unreal deep blue. The forest
caught its breath in fear as she approached, strange little

sounds could be heard from under the moss, branches rustled with fright and the lights of tiny eyes went out everywhere. Without pausing, she went up to the top of the cliff overlooking the southern shore and gazed out over the sea, now growing dark as night fell.

She could see the hurricane lamp at the top of the mast of the *Adventure* quite clearly, a lonely star gliding past the last islands, all the time moving farther out towards the open sea.

She gazed at it for a long time, for she was never in a hurry. Time for her was endless and passed very slowly. Time for her contained nothing, except the occasional lamps which were lit as autumn approached.

Now she glided down the ravine towards the beach. Behind her she left big shapeless footprints, as though a seal had dragged itself to the edge of the water. The waves drew back as she approached, and then hesitated as if they didn't know what to do next. The water became smooth and still round the dark hem of her skirt and began to freeze.

For a long time she stood there, while a cloud of freezing mist gathered around her. Now and then she slowly lifted one of her feet, and the ice crackled and became thicker and thicker. She was building an island of ice for herself in order to reach the hurricane lamp. It was out of sight behind the islands now, but she knew it was there somewhere. If it went out before she got to it, it wouldn't matter. She could wait. They would light another lamp some other evening. They always did sooner or later.

*   *   *

Moominpappa was steering the boat. He held the rudder tightly in one of his paws, feeling that he and the boat understood each other. He was completely at peace with himself. His family looked just as tiny and helpless as they had

looked in the crystal ball; he was guiding them safely across
the vast ocean through the silent, blue night. The hurricane
lamp lit the way, just as if Moominpappa had drawn a firm
bright line across the map, saying: "from here . . . to there.
That's where we're going to live. There my lighthouse will
be the centre of the world, it will tower proudly above the
dangers of the ocean at its feet."

"You don't feel the cold, do you?" he shouted happily.
"Have you wrapped the blanket round you?" he asked
Moominmamma. "Look, we've left the last island behind us
now, and soon it will be the darkest part of the night. Sailing
at night is very difficult. You have to be on the look-out all
the time."

"Why of course, dear!" said Moominmamma, who was
lying curled up in the bottom of the boat. "This is all a
great experience," she thought. The blanket had got a little
wet and she moved gingerly towards the windward side. But
the ribs of the boat got in the way of her ears all the time.

Little My sat in the bow of the boat, humming monoton-
ously to herself.

"Mamma," whispered Moomintroll. "What happened
to her to make her like that?"

"Who?"

"The Groke. Did somebody do something to her to make
her so awful?"

"No one knows," said Moominmamma, drawing her tail
out of the water. "It was probably because nobody did
anything at all. Nobody bothered about her, I mean. I don't
suppose she remembers anyway, and I don't suppose she
goes around thinking about it either. She's like the rain or
the darkness, or a stone you have to walk round if you want
to get past. Do you want some coffee? There's some in the
thermos in the white basket."

"Not just now," said Moomintroll. "She's got glassy eyes just like a fish. Can she talk?"

Moominmamma sighed and said: "No one talks to her, or about her either, otherwise she gets bigger and starts to chase one. And you mustn't feel sorry for her. You seem to imagine that she longs for everything that's alight, but all she really wants to do is to sit on it so that it'll go out and never burn again. And now I think I might go to sleep for a while."

Pale autumn stars had come out all over the sky. Moomintroll lay on his back looking at the hurricane lamp, but he was thinking about the Groke. If she was someone you mustn't talk to or about, then she would gradually vanish and not even dare to believe in her own existence. He wondered whether a mirror might help. With lots and lots of mirrors one could be any number of people, seen from the front and from the back, and perhaps these people might even talk to each other. Perhaps . . .

Everything was silent. The rudder creaked softly, and they all slept. Moominpappa was alone with his family. He was wide-awake, more wide-awake than he had ever been before.

      *   *   *

Far away, the Groke decided towards morning that she would set off. The island under her was black and transparent with a sharp bowsprit of ice pointing south. She gathered up her dark skirts, hanging round her like the leaves of a faded rose. They opened out and rustled, lifting themselves like wings. So the Groke's slow journey over the sea began.

She moved her skirts upwards, outwards and downwards, like slow swimming-strokes, in the frozen air. The water drew back in scared, choppy waves, and she floated on into the dawn with a cloud of drifting snow behind her. Against the horizon she looked like a large reeling bat. She found it slow-going, but somehow she managed. She had time. She had nothing else but time.

*   *   *

The family continued all night and all the next day until it was night again. Moominpappa still sat at the rudder waiting to catch sight of his lighthouse. But the night was just deep blue, and no lighthouse could be seen flashing on the horizon.

"We're on the right course," said Moominpappa. "I know we're set on the right course. With this wind we ought to get there by midnight, but we should have seen the lighthouse when it began to get dark."

"Maybe some rotter's put it out," suggested Little My.

"Do you think anyone would put a lighthouse out," said Moominpappa. "You can depend on it that the lighthouse is working all right. There are some things one can be absolutely sure of: sea currents, the seasons, the rising of the sun, for example. And that lighthouses always work, too."

"We shall see it soon," said Moominmamma. Her head was full of little thoughts that she couldn't really get organised. "I do hope it's working," she thought. "He's so happy. I do hope there really is a lighthouse somewhere out there, and not just a bit of fly-dirt after all. We can't possibly go home now, particularly after such a grand start . . . You can find big pink shells, but the white ones look very nice against black soil. I wonder whether the roses will grow out there . . ."

"Shush! I can hear something," said Little My from the bow. "Be quiet all of you! Something's happening."

They all lifted their noses and stared into the night. The sound of oars reached their ears. The unknown boat gradually came nearer, gliding out of the darkness. It was a little grey boat, and the man rowing it was resting on his oars looking at them quite undismayed. He looked very scruffy, but appeared to be quite calm. The light shone on his large blue eyes, which were as transparent as water. He had some fishing-rods in the bow of his boat.

"Do the fish bite at night?" asked Moominpappa.

The fisherman turned and looked straight past them. He wasn't going to say anything.

"Isn't there an island with a big lighthouse somewhere near here?" Moominpappa continued. "Why isn't it working? We ought to have seen it a long time ago."

The fisherman glided past them in his boat. They could hardly hear him when he finally said something. "Can't say, really . . . Go back home . . . You've come too far . . ."

He disappeared behind them. They listened for the sound of his oars, but could hear nothing in the silent night.

"He was a little odd, wasn't he?" said Moominpappa uncertainly.

"Very odd, if you ask me," said Little My. "Quite nuts."

Moominmamma sighed and tried to straighten her legs. "But so are most of the people we know—more or less," she said.

The wind had dropped. Moominpappa sat bolt upright at the rudder with his nose in the air. "Now," he said, "I have a feeling we're there. We're coming in on the leeward side of the island. But I just don't understand why the lighthouse isn't working."

The air was warm and full of the scent of heather. Everything was completely still. And then out of the night loomed an enormous shadow: the island itself was towering over them, looking at them carefully. They could feel its hot breath as the boat struck the sandy beach and came to a standstill: they felt they were being watched, and huddled together, not daring to move.

"Did you hear that, Mamma," whispered Moomintroll.

Swift feet galloped up the beach, splashed a little, and then everything was quiet again.

"It was only Little My going ashore," said Moominmamma. She shook herself, as though to break the silence, and began to poke about among her baskets, trying to get the box of earth with her roses over the side of the boat.

"Now, take it easy," said Moominpappa nervously. "I'll look after all this. Everything must be properly organised from the beginning. The boat is always the most important

thing . . . You sit still and take it easy."

Moominmamma sat down obediently, trying not to get in the way of the sail as it came down, and the boom as it swung backwards and forwards, while Moominpappa scrambled about in the boat organising things. The hurricane lamp lit up a circle of white sand and black water, and outside it there was nothing but darkness. Moominpappa and Moomintroll dragged the mattress ashore but not without getting one corner of it wet. The boat heeled over and the blue trunk pressed the rose-bushes against the side of the boat.

Moominmamma sat waiting with her nose in her paws. Everything was as it should be. In time she would probably get used to being looked after, perhaps she would come to like it. Even now she slept for a moment or two.

There was Moominpappa standing in the water and saying to her: "You can get out now. Everything's ready." He was happy and wide-awake, and his hat was pushed right back. Higher up on the beach he had built a tent of the sails and the oars, looking like a big, squatting animal. Moominmamma tried to see whether there were any shells on this new beach of theirs, but it was much too dark. They had promised her that there would be shells, big and rare ones such as are to be found far out to sea.

"Here you are," said Moominpappa. "Now all you have to do is to sleep. I shall stand guard outside all night, so there's no need for you to be afraid. Tomorrow night you will be able to sleep in my lighthouse. If only I understood why it isn't working . . . Is it nice and cosy inside there?"

"It's just fine!" said Moominmamma, creeping in under the sail.

Little My was off somewhere on her own as usual. It didn't matter, really, as she was the one member of the family who seemed to manage all right by herself. Everything seemed to be going well.

Moomintroll watched Moominmamma turn round once or twice on the damp mattress until she found her favourite spot, give a little sigh and fall asleep. Of all strange things, that was the strangest, the way Moominmamma could sleep in this new place without unpacking, without making their beds and without giving them a sweet before they went to sleep. She had even left her handbag behind her on the sand. It was a little bit frightening in a way, but at the same time cheering; it meant that all this was a real change, and not just an adventure.

Moomintroll lifted his nose and peeped out from under the sail. There sat Moominpappa on guard, with the hurricane lamp in front of him. He cast a very large, long shadow; the whole of him looked much larger than usual. Moomintroll rolled himself into a ball again and put his paws under his warm tummy. He gave himself up to his dreams. They were blue and rocking, like the sea had been that night.

Gradually the morning came. Moominpappa was quite alone with his island, and with each hour that passed it became more and more his very own. The sky began to grow pale and the rocks rose up in front of him in great undulating masses, and above them he could see the lighthouse. There it was at last, huge and black against the grey of the sky. It was much bigger than he had imagined it would be, for it was just the time when the first light makes one feel helpless and everything seems dangerous if one is alone and awake all by oneself.

Moominpappa turned out the hurricane lamp and made the beach disappear. He didn't want the lighthouse to see him yet. A cold early morning wind blew in from the sea, and he could hear the cries of sea-gulls from somewhere on the other side of the island.

As Moominpappa sat on the beach, the lighthouse seemed to rise higher and higher above him. It was just like his model that he hadn't had time to finish. Now he could see that the roof wasn't as pointed as he had thought and that there was no rail. He gazed at the dark and deserted lighthouse for a long time, and gradually it began to grow smaller and more like the picture he had carried in his mind for so long.

"In any case, it's mine," he thought, and lit his pipe. "I'll capture the lighthouse. I'll present it to my family and say: 'This is where you're going to live. When we are safe inside, nothing dangerous can happen to us'."

*   *   *

Little My sat on the lighthouse steps watching the dawn. Below her, the island lay in the half-light, looking like a big grey cat stretching itself, with its claws spread out; both its paws were resting in the sea and its tail was a long, narrow point at the other end of the island. The cat's back was bristling, but its eyes were invisible.

"Huh!" said Little My. "This is no ordinary island. It goes down to the bottom of the sea quite differently from other islands. I bet things'll happen here!"

She huddled up and waited. The sun came up over the sea
and shadows and colours began to appear. The island began
to take shape and draw in its claws. Everything began to
shine, and the chalk-white gulls circled over the point. The
cat vanished. But right across the island lay the shadow of
the lighthouse like a broad dark ribbon stretching down to
the beach where the boat was.

There they all were, far below her like small ants. Moominpappa and Moomintroll carrying as much as they could,
striding out of the alder bushes and into the shadow of the
lighthouse. There they became even smaller, and stopped,
three little white dots turning their noses upwards to look
at what was above them.

"Oh! how big it is!" said Moominmamma, and froze to
the spot.

"Big?" shouted Moominpappa. "It's enormous! It's
probably the biggest lighthouse that was ever built. And do
you realise that this is the very last island, nobody lives
beyond it—there's nothing but sea. We're looking the sea
straight in the face, so to speak, and far behind us are all
those people who live on islands much nearer to the mainland. It's a wonderful thought, don't you think?"

"Yes, wonderful, Pappa!" Moomintroll cried.

"Can't I carry the basket for a while," Mamma asked.

"No, no," said Moominpappa. "You're not to carry a
thing. All you've got to do is to walk straight into your new
house—but wait, you must have some flowers to take in with
you—wait a moment . . ." He disappeared in among the
poplar trees and began to pick some flowers.

Moominmamma looked around. How poor the soil was!
And there were so many stones everywhere, masses of them
all over the place. It certainly wasn't going to be an easy
matter to make a garden there.

"What a sad sound, Mamma," said Moomintroll. "What is it?"

Moominmamma listened. "Yes, it is," she said. "It does sound sad. But it's only the aspens, they always sound like that."

Tiny wind-swept aspens were growing between the stones, their leaves rustling in the gentle breeze blowing off the sea. They were trembling violently, and one shudder after another passed through them.

The island was different by day; it seemed to have turned its back on them. It wasn't looking at them the way it had during the warmth of the night; instead it was gazing far out to sea.

"Here you are," said Moominpappa. "They're terribly small, but they'll open all right if you put them in the sun. Now we must push on. Soon there'll be a proper path from the beach right up to the house. And there'll be a jetty for the

boat. There's so much to be done here! Just think! Fancy being able to build all one's life and turn the island into a miracle of perfection!'' He picked up the baskets and hurried on ahead through the heather towards the lighthouse.

In front of them lay age-old rocks with steep and sharp sides and they stumbled past precipice after precipice, grey and full of crevices and fissures.

"Everything's much too big here," thought Moominmamma. "Or perhaps I'm too small."

Only the path was as small and insecure as she was. They groped their way forward together through the boulders and came to the rock where the lighthouse stood, waiting on its heavy feet of concrete.

"Welcome home!" said Moominpappa.

Slowly they turned their gaze to the lighthouse. Higher and higher—it seemed to go on forever, white and gigantic, it was simply unbelievable. Right at the top, a cloud of frightened swallows flew dizzily backwards and forwards.

"I feel a little seasick," said Moominmamma weakly.

Moomintroll looked at his father. Moominpappa climbed solemnly up the lighthouse steps and lifted his paw to take hold of the door.

"It's locked," said Little My behind him.

Moominpappa turned round and stared at her blankly.

"It's locked," repeated Little My. "There's no key."

Moominpappa pulled the door. He twisted and turned, he knocked and even gave it a kick. Finally, he took a step backwards and looked at it.

"Here's the nail," he said. "Quite obviously a nail for the key. You can see it is! I've never heard of anyone who locked a door without hanging the key properly on the nail. Particularly a lighthouse-keeper."

"Perhaps it's under the steps," said Moominmamma.

It wasn't under the steps.

"Now everybody keep quiet. Quite quiet. I must have time to think." He went and sat on the rock a little way away with his nose pointing out to sea.

It was warmer now, and the south-west wind blew gently over the island. It was the right day, the perfect day for occupying a lighthouse. Moominpappa was so disappointed, he felt a sinking feeling in his stomach and he couldn't collect his thoughts. There was no other place for a key than the nail or under the steps. There were no door-frames and no window-ledges, no flat stones in front of the steps. Everything was smooth and bare.

Moominpappa's brain felt tired. He was conscious all the time that his family was standing behind him, waiting in silence for him to say something. Finally he called over his shoulder: "I'm going to sleep for a while. Problems often solve themselves while one sleeps. The brain works better if one leaves it in peace." He rolled himself up in a crevice in the rock and pulled his hat over his eyes. With a great sense of relief, he fell asleep.

Moomintroll went and looked underneath the steps. "There's nothing here except a dead bird," he said. It was a tiny, frail skeleton, quite white. He laid it on the steps, where it was immediately blown down the rock by the wind.

"I saw lots of those down there in the heather," said Little My, immediately interested. "Reminds me of 'The Revenge of the Forgotten Bones'; jolly good story that."

They stood in silence for a while.

"What do we do now?" asked Moomintroll.

"I was thinking about that fisherman we met during the night," said Moominmamma. "He must live somewhere on the island. Perhaps he knows something." She opened the sack with the bedding in it and took out the red blanket.

"Cover Pappa up with this," she said. "It isn't good to sleep on the rock like that. And then you can go round the island and look for the fisherman. Bring me a little sea-water on your way back, there's a good troll. The copper can is in the boat. And the potatoes, too."

It was nice to get moving and have something to do. Moomintroll turned his back on the lighthouse and wandered away across the island. A sea of red heather covered the slope, and below the rock it was warm and peaceful. The ground was hard and hot. It smelt good, but not at all like the garden at home.

Now that he was alone, Moomintroll could begin to look at the island and smell it in the right way. He could feel it with his paws, prick up his ears and listen to it. Away from the roar of the sea the island was quieter than the valley at home, completely silent and terribly, terribly old.

"It isn't an island that'll be easy to get to know," Moomintroll thought. "It wants to be left in peace."

The heather disappeared in a mossy swamp in the middle of the island, came out the other side, only to vanish in a low thicket of spruce and dwarf birch. It was odd that there wasn't a single tall tree. Everything seemed to grow so close to the ground, groping its way across the rock. It occurred to Moomintroll that he, too, should make himself as small as he could. He began to run towards the point.

★   ★   ★

Far out on the western end of the island stood a little house made of stone and cement. It was fixed firmly to the rock with lots of iron clamps. Its back was round like a seal's, and it looked straight out to sea through a tiny substantial window-pane. The house was so small that you could just about sit in it if you were the right size, and the fisherman had built it for himself. He was lying on his back with his arms under his head, gazing at a cloud moving slowly across the sky.

"Good morning," said Moomintroll. "Is this where you live?"

"Only when it's stormy," replied the fisherman vaguely.

Moomintroll nodded seriously. It was just the right way to live if one liked big waves. Sitting in the middle of the breakers, watching the waves as high as mountains coming and going and listening to the sea thundering on the roof. Moomintroll wanted to ask: "Can I come and watch the waves sometime?" But this house was obviously built just for one.

"Mamma sends her compliments," he said. "She asked me to inquire about the key of the lighthouse."

The fisherman made no answer.

"Pappa can't get in," Moomintroll explained. "We thought that perhaps you might know where . . ."

Silence. More clouds appeared in the sky.

"There *was* a lighthouse-keeper, wasn't there?" Moomintroll asked.

At last the fisherman turned his head and looked at him with his watery-blue eyes.

"No. I don't know anything about a key," he said.

"Did he put the light out and go away?" continued Moomintroll. He had never met anybody before who didn't answer when asked a question. It worried him and made him feel uncomfortable.

"I can't really remember," said the fisherman. "I've forgotten what he looked like . . ." He got up slowly and pottered off over the rock, grey and wrinkled and as light as a feather. He was very small and had not the slightest desire to talk to anyone.

Moomintroll stood watching the fisherman for a while, then turned and walked back across the narrow strip of land. He went in the direction of the beach where the boat was in order to fetch the copper can. They would be eating soon, and Moominmamma would make a fire between some stones and lay the meal out on the steps of the lighthouse. Then somehow or other things would be all right.

*   *   *

The beach was full of completely white sand. The bay was like a half-moon stretching from one headland to the other, and it formed a trap for all that the winds swept round the island towards the leeward side. Drift-wood lay piled up at the high-water mark under the alder bushes, but lower down on the beach the sand was empty and as smooth as a polished floor. It was nice to walk on. If you walked along the edge of the water, your paws left little holes that filled up immediately, like springs. Moomintroll started to look for shells for his mother, but the only ones he could see were broken. Perhaps they'd been smashed by the sea.

He saw something shining in the sand that wasn't a shell. It was a tiny little silver horseshoe. Quite close by there were hoof-marks in the sand, leading straight into the sea.

"A horse must have jumped into the sea just here and lost one of his shoes," Moomintroll observed to himself seriously. "That's what it must be. A very tiny horse indeed. I wonder whether it's made of real silver, or only silver-plate?" He picked up the horseshoe and decided that he would give it to his mother.

A little further on, the hoof-marks came out of the sea and went straight up the beach. "It must be a sea-horse—I've never seen one of those. I know you can only find them far out to sea where the water is terribly deep. I hope this sea-horse has a spare pair of shoes at home," Moomintroll thought.

The boat lay on her side with her sail rolled up, looking as though she never wanted to sail again. She had been pulled so high up the beach that she seemed to have nothing to do with the sea any more. Moomintroll stood still and looked at the *Adventure*. "I do feel sorry for her," he thought, "but perhaps she's asleep. Anyway, we shall be putting a net out one of these nights."

The clouds were coming up over the island, calm blue-grey clouds in parallel lines across the sky, stretching right to the horizon. The beach seemed very lonely. "I'm going home," thought Moomintroll. Home for him suddenly meant the steps in front of the lighthouse. The valley where they had lived seemed a long way away. Besides, he had found a silver horseshoe that belonged to a sea-horse. Somehow that settled the matter.

*   *   *

"But he can't have forgotten everything!" said Moomin-pappa, for the second time. "He must have known the lighthouse-keeper. They lived on the same island. They must have been friends!"

"He doesn't remember a thing," said Moomintroll.

Little My breathed in through her nose, and then breathed out between her teeth.

"That old fisherman is an old fool with a head full of sea-weed. I knew it as soon as I set eyes on him. If two men like that live on the same island, either they know all there is to know about each other or else they don't want to have anything to do with each other at all. Probably both. One as a result of the other, I mean. Believe you me, I know. I'm pretty sharp when it comes to things like that."

"I do hope it doesn't rain," murmured Moominmamma.

They stood round Moomintroll in a circle. It was quite chilly now that the sun was behind the clouds. Moomintroll felt a little confused and didn't want to tell them about the house built for looking at the waves. And it was quite impossible to give Moominmamma the horseshoe just then, with them all standing and staring at him like that. He made up his mind to give it to her later when they were alone.

"I do hope it doesn't rain," Moominmamma repeated. She carried the copper can to the fireplace and put the flowers Moominpappa had picked for her in water. "If it rains," she said, "I ought to scrub one of the pots to collect rain-water in. That is if there are any pots here . . ."

"But I'm the one who's going to do all that sort of thing," exclaimed Moominpappa plaintively. "Just be patient. Everything must be done in the right order. We can't bother about food and rain and small trifles like that before I've found the key."

"Huh!" said Little My. "That old fisherman has thrown the key into the sea, and the lighthouse-keeper along with it. Frightful things have happened here, and there's worse to come!"

Moominpappa sighed. He went round the lighthouse to the rocks overlooking the sea, where the others couldn't see him. The family got on his nerves at times—they could never stick to the matter in hand. He wondered whether all fathers

found the same thing.

Well, there was no point in searching for the key or trying to produce it by going to sleep. He must *feel* where it was. He must try getting in the right mood, like his father-in-law used to do. All her life, his mother-in-law had gone round dropping things everywhere or leaving them behind and forgetting where she had left them. Then his father-in-law would turn on something in his brain. That's all that was needed. He always found things after that. Then he used to say· "Here's your old junk," but in a kind way.

Moominpappa tried. He sauntered about aimlessly among the rocks and tried to turn something on in his brain. In the end he felt that everything he had up there was rattling about like peas in a tin. But nothing happened.

His paws had found a well-worn path that twisted in and out of the boulders in the short sunburnt grass. While he was walking and trying to turn something on in his brain, it occurred to him that perhaps it was the lighthouse-keeper who had gone up and down this path. He must have gone up and down here many times a long time ago. And he must have come to exactly the same spot on the cliffs overlooking the sea where Moominpappa had come to. The path came to an end. Here there was nothing but the great empty sea.

Moominpappa went up to the edge and looked over. Here the cliff fell away in precipice after precipice, a mass of playful dancing lines and curves that bent out of sight deep, deep down. At the foot of the cliff he could hear the murmur of the breakers, the water rose and fell, heaved against the rocks and then sank back like a clumsy great beast. The water lay in the shadow, and it was very dark.

Moominpappa's legs trembled and he felt distinctly giddy. He sat down quickly, but he couldn't stop himself looking down. This was the great ocean, who knows how many fathoms deep, and it was quite unlike the sea and the waves that played round the jetty back there at home. Moominpappa leant a little further forward and caught sight of a little ledge just beneath the crest. It seemed quite natural to let oneself slide down to the smooth shelf in the cliff-face, it was hollowed out and as round as a chair. Suddenly Moominpappa was completely alone and cut off; there was nothing but sky and sea around him.

This is where the lighthouse-keeper must have sat. He must have sat there often. Moominpappa shut his eyes. Everything around him was so huge that he felt giddy, and the peas in his head rattled worse than ever. The lighthouse-keeper must have come down here when a high sea was running . . . He had seen the gulls flying in the wind against a stormy sky, like a cloud of snow in front of his eyes. Drops of water, like little pearls, had reached him, hanging suspended for a moment in the air in front of him before plunging down

into the thundering black water down there . . .

Moominpappa opened his eyes and shook himself. He pressed his back and his paws against the wall of rock behind him, where he could see that little white flowers were growing in the cracks in the rock. Imagine! Flowers! And in the widest crack there was something shining rust-red; a key, a heavy iron key.

Something clicked inside Moominpappa's head. Of course, everything was as clear as day. This was the place where the lighthouse-keeper came when he wanted to be entirely alone. A place for thought and meditation. And it was here that he had left the key so that Moominpappa should find it and take over the lighthouse. With great ceremony and the help of magic forces, Moominpappa had been chosen as the owner of the lighthouse and its keeper.

*   *   *

"Oh, how wonderful! You've found it then!" said Moominmamma.

"Where was it?" exclaimed Moomintroll.

"Oh, I don't really know," said Moominpappa mysteriously. "The world is full of great and wonderful things for those who are ready for them. Perhaps it was the biggest and whitest gull that presented it to me . . ."

"Huh!" said Little My. "On a silk ribbon, with a military band playing, I suppose."

Moominpappa went up the steps and put the key in the

lock. Slowly and with a great deal of creaking the huge door opened. Inside all was darkness. Little My dashed in like a flash, but Moominpappa caught her by the hair and pulled her back. "Oh no you don't!" he said. "You shan't be first this time. I'm the lighthouse-keeper now, and I must go in first and carry out an inspection." He disappeared into the darkness with Little My at his heels.

Moominmamma came slowly up to the door, and looked in. The lighthouse was quite hollow, like a rotten tree trunk, and from top to bottom there was a rickety winding staircase. With what seemed like an awful effort, the staircase climbed up and up in smaller and smaller spirals, creaking and groaning as Moominpappa went up it. A little daylight filtered through holes in the thick walls, and in each hole the silhouette of a large, motionless bird could be seen. The birds stared down at them.

"You must remember that it's cloudy," whispered Moomintroll. "You know that everything looks a little gloomy when the sun's not shining."

"Of course," said Moominmamma. She stepped over the threshold and stopped. It was very cold and damp inside. Between the puddles of water the ground was dark and wet, and a few planks had been put down to get to the stairs. Moominmamma hesitated.

"Look!" said Moomintroll. "I've got something for you."

Moominmamma took the silver horseshoe, and looked at it for a long time.

"It's beautiful!" she said. "What a lovely present! I never knew that such small horses existed . . ."

"Come along in, Mamma," called Moomintroll. "Come in and we'll run right to the top!"

*   *   *

Moominpappa was standing in the doorway at the top, wearing an entirely different hat. It had a soft, floppy brim and a lumpy crown.

"What do you think of it?" he said. "I found it on a nail inside the door. It must have belonged to the lighthouse-keeper. Come in! Come in! Everything's exactly as I imagined it would be."

It was a large round room, with a low ceiling and four windows. In the middle of the floor there was an unpainted table and some empty boxes. Over by the fireplace stood a bed and a little desk. An iron ladder led up to a trap-door in the ceiling.

"Up there is the light," explained Moominpappa. "I shall light it this evening. Isn't it lovely to have such white walls? It makes the room seem so big and airy. If you look out of the window it's the same—big and free and airy!"

He looked at Moominmamma, who began to laugh, saying: "You're quite right! It's overpoweringly big and airy up here!"

"Someone's got real mad in here," observed Little My. The floor was covered with splinters of glass and above them on the white wall there was an oily stain which had run down the wall forming a pool on the floor below it.

"I wonder who broke his lamp," said Moominmamma, picking up a brass lamp-holder which had rolled under the table. "And then had to sit here in the dark." She ran her paws over the top of the table. Its surface was covered with hundreds, perhaps thousands of tiny scratches, six in a row, with the seventh drawn straight through the others. Seven? There were seven days in a week. Week after week, all the same, except one which had only five scratches. Moomin-mamma continued her inspection. She picked up cups and saucepans, read what was written on the empty boxes: raisins from Malaga, whisky from Scotland, and ordinary Finnish crisp-bread; she lifted the blankets on the bed and saw that there were still sheets underneath, but she didn't open the desk.

The others looked at her in suspense. Finally, Moominpappa said: "Well?"

"He must have been a very lonely man," said Moominmamma.

"Yes, but what do you *think* of it?"

"I think it's very nice here," said Moominmamma. "We can all live together in the same room."

"Yes, that's it!" exclaimed Moominpappa. "I'll collect some drift-wood from the beach and build beds for us all. I'll make a path and a jetty—there's so much to be done here . . . But first we must bring in the luggage in case it rains. No, no. Not you, dear. You must take things easy and feel yourself at home."

Little My turned in the doorway and said: "I'm going to sleep outside. I don't want a bed, beds are stupid."

"All right, dear," said Moominmamma. "You can come inside if it starts raining."

When Moominmamma was alone, she hung up the silver horseshoe on a nail above the door. Then she went over to the window and looked out. She went from one window to another. Sea everywhere, nothing but sea and the cries of swallows. The mainland wasn't visible at all.

In the last window she found an indelible pencil, some bits of string and a needle for mending fishing-nets. She stood playing with the pencil. Absent-mindedly, she started to draw a little flower on the window-sill, shading in the leaves nicely, but not thinking about anything in particular.

*   *   *

Moominpappa stood in the fireplace with his head up the chimney. "There's a bird's nest here," he shouted. "That's why it won't burn."

"Are there any birds in it?" Moominmamma asked.

Moominpappa was quite black when he emerged from the chimney. "Some poor little bald coot, I expect," he said. "But she isn't at home. She's probably flown south."

"But she'll be back in the spring!" exclaimed Moomintroll. "She must be able to find her nest when she comes home. We can cook outdoors!"

"What? For the rest of our lives?" asked Little My.

"Well, we could move the nest after a while," Moomintroll muttered.

"Huh! Typical!" said Little My. "Do you think the bald coot will know whether her nest has been moved immediately or only after a little while? You only say that so you can chuck her out with a clear conscience."

"Shall we really eat outdoors for the rest of our lives?" Moominpappa asked in amazement. They all looked at Moominmamma.

"Take it down," she said. "We can hang it out of the window. Sometimes trolls are more important than bald coots."

     ★   ★   ★

Moominmamma pushed the dirty dishes under the bed to make the room tidier, and then she went out to look for soil.

She stopped by the lighthouse steps to throw a little sea-water on the rose-bush. It was still waiting in its box with the earth from home. The garden must be made on the leeward side and it must be as near the lighthouse as possible, where it would get the sun most of the day. But above all, it should have plenty of deep, rich soil.

Moominmamma looked and looked. She searched along the rock where the lighthouse stood, through the heather down towards the moss, she went into the aspen thicket, she wandered over the warm peaty ground, but there was still no soil anywhere.

She had never seen so many stones before. Behind the clump of aspen trees there was nothing but stones, a desert of round grey stones. In the middle of them someone had lifted some up, making a hole. Moominmamma went and looked into the hole, but there was nothing but more stones in it, just as grey and just as round. She wondered what the

lighthouse-keeper had been looking for. Nothing in particular, perhaps. Maybe he had done it just to amuse himself. He had picked up one stone after another, but they had rolled back and he had got tired of the whole thing and walked away.

Moominmamma went on towards the sandy beach. Down there she found soil at last. A dark belt of rich soil lay along the line of the beach under the alders. Tough green plants were growing between the stones, opening in bursts of gold and violet, a sudden jungle of richness.

Moominmamma dug her paws in the ground. She could feel that it was full of millions of growing roots that mustn't be disturbed. But it didn't matter, there was soil after all. Now for the first time she felt that the island was real.

She called to Moominpappa, who was collecting pieces of wood in the seaweed, ran towards him with her apron waving in the wind, and shouted: "I've found soil! I've found soil!"

Moominpappa looked up. "Hallo there!" he said. "What do you think of my island?"

"It's not like anything else in the world!" Moominmamma assured him enthusiastically. "The soil's down on the beach instead of somewhere in the middle of the island!"

"I'll explain it for you," said Moominpappa. "You must always ask me if there's anything you don't understand—I know about everything connected with the sea. It's like this: what you found was seaweed thrown up by the waves. After a time it becomes soil, real soil. Didn't you know that?" Moominpappa laughed, and with his paws outstretched he seemed to be giving her all the seaweed in the sea.

Moominmamma started to gather seaweed. She carried it all day, laying it in a crevice in the rock. She would have a patch of garden there by and by. The seaweed had the same

warm, dark colour as the soil back home, and its very own touch of purple and orange as well.

Moominmamma felt calm and happy. She dreamed of carrots, radishes and potatoes, and of how they grew fat and round in the warm soil. She could see green leaves appearing in strong, healthy clusters. She saw them waving in the wind against the blue sea, heavy with tomatoes, peas and beans for the family to eat. She knew that none of this would come true until the following summer, but it didn't matter. She had something to dream about. And deep down inside she dreamed most of all of having an apple tree.

The day was coming to a close. The sound of the hammer up in the lighthouse had stopped long ago, and the swallows were much quieter now. Moominmamma whistled to herself as she walked home through the heather, her arms full of drift-wood. Moominpappa had built a hand-rail for her to hold on to, and there were two little beds made of wood in front of the doorway. There was a barrel he had found in the sea, too. It was quite whole, and looked as though it had been green once.

Somehow, the winding staircase was less frightening now. You just had to be careful not to look down, and it was best to think about something else. Moomintroll was sitting at the table, arranging small round pebbles in little heaps.

"Hallo," said Moominmamma. "Where's Pappa?"

"He's up above, lighting the lamp," Moomintroll answered. "I wasn't allowed to go up with him. He's been there an awful long time."

The empty bird's nest stood on top of the desk. Mamma went on whistling as she piled up the wood by the stove. The wind had died down and the sun was shining through the western window, throwing a warm light over the floor and the white wall.

When the fire was beginning to glow, Little My crept in through the door and jumped up on the window-sill like a cat. She pressed her nose against the window-pane and made ugly faces at the swallows.

Suddenly the trap-door opened with a loud noise and Moominpappa climbed down the iron ladder.

"Is it burning well?" asked Moominmamma. "You've made some lovely beds for us. And I thought that barrel would be just the thing for salt fish. It seems a pity to use it only for rain-water . . ."

Moominpappa went to the window facing south and peered out. Moominmamma looked up quickly and noticed that his tail was quite stiff and the end of it was wagging with irritation. She put some more wood on the fire and opened a tin of herrings. Moominpappa drank his tea without saying a word. When Moominmamma had cleared away, she put the hurricane lamp on the table and said: "I remember hearing once that some lighthouses use gas. When the gas is finished it's quite impossible to light them."

Moominpappa got up from the table crying: "But you don't understand, I'm the lighthouse-keeper now! The lamp must be alight! It's the whole point. Do you think one

can live in a lighthouse without keeping the lamp alight?
What would happen to all the boats out there in the dark.
They could go aground and sink in front of our very eyes at
any moment . . ."

"He's right," said Little My. "And in the morning the
beach would be full of drowned Fillyjonks, Mymbles and
Whompses, all pale in the face and green with seaweed . . ."

"Don't be silly," said Moominmamma. She turned to
Moominpappa and said. "If you can't get it to light this
evening, you will tomorrow, or some other day. And if it
won't work at all, we'll hang the hurricane lamp in the
window if the weather's bad. Somebody's bound to see it
and understand that if they sail in this direction they'll go
aground. From one thing to another, don't you think it
would be a good idea to carry the beds up before it gets dark?
I don't trust those rickety stairs."

"I'll carry them up on my own," said Moominpappa,
taking his hat off its nail.

*   *   *

Out on the rock it was almost dark. Moominpappa stood
watching the sea. "Now she's lighting the hurricane lamp,"
he thought. "She's turning up the flame and standing there
looking at it as she always does. We've got plenty of
paraffin . . ."

All the birds had gone to sleep. The rocks at the western
end of the island looked black against the sky where the sun
had gone down. One of them had a beacon on it, or perhaps
it was a cairn of stones. Moominpappa lifted up the first bed,
then stopped and listened.

Far away he could hear a faint wailing sound, a strange,
lonely shriek unlike anything he had heard before. It seemed
to come to him across the water, a vast desolate waste. For a

moment, Moominpappa thought he felt the rock trembling under him, but then everything was quiet again.

"It must have been a bird," he thought. "They have very strange cries." He lifted the bed on to his shoulders. It was a good firm bed, and there wasn't anything wrong with it. But the lighthouse-keeper's bed up in the tower was his, and none of the others would use it.

*   *   *

Moominpappa dreamed that he was running up some stairs that never seemed to come to an end. The darkness surrounding him was full of the flapping of birds' wings, birds that escaped silently. The staircase creaked with every step he made, and groaned loudly. He was in a terrible hurry. He had to get to the top to light the lamp before it was too late, it seemed desperately important that he should get it to work. The stairs got narrower and narrower. Now he was conscious of the sound of iron under his paws, he was up where the lamp was waiting for him in its round house of glass. The dream got slower as Moominpappa groped round the walls looking for matches. Great pieces of curved coloured glass were in his way, reflecting the sea outside. The red glass made the waves as red as fire, and through the green glass the sea suddenly turned emerald-green, a sea that seemed cold and remote as though it were miles away on the moon, or perhaps nowhere at all. There was no time to lose, but the more he hurried, the slower things seemed to become. He stumbled over the cylinders of gas which rolled away across the floor, more and more of them, like waves. Then the birds returned and beat their wings against the glass. Everything prevented him from lighting the lamp. Moominpappa shouted loudly with fright. The glass broke and fell round him in a thousand shining splinters, and the sea rose high above the roof of the lighthouse, and he started to fall, deeper and deeper—and woke up in the middle of the floor with his blanket round his head.

"What's the matter?" said Moominmamma.

The room was still and blue, with its four windows outlining the night.

"I was dreaming," said Moominpappa. "It was awful."

Moominmamma got up and put a few dry sticks on the glowing ashes of the fire. It burst into flame, and a warm golden light flickered in the darkness.

"I'll make you a sandwich," she said. "It's because you're sleeping in a strange place."

Moominpappa sat on the edge of the bed and ate his sandwich and his frightening dream began to disappear.

"I don't think it's the room," he said. "It's this bed that makes one have such nightmares. I'll make myself a new one."

"I think you're right," said Moominmamma. "Have you missed anything? One can't hear the trees in the forest any more."

Moominpappa listened. He could hear the sound of the sea murmuring round the island, and remembered how the trees used to whisper round their old home at night.

"Actually it's rather pleasant," said Moominmamma, drawing the blanket up round her ears. "It's different. You won't have any more terrible dreams, will you?"

"I don't expect so. A sandwich *does* taste good in the middle of the night!"

The West Wind

Moomintroll and Little My lay on their stomachs in the sun
looking into the thicket. It was low and tangled; tiny angry-
looking spruce trees and even smaller birches battling with
the wind all their lives. They grew very close together for
protection. The tops of the trees had stopped growing, but
the branches held on tight to the ground wherever they
could reach it.

"Who would have thought they could be so ferocious,"
said Little My, full of admiration.

Moomintroll peeped under the thick mass of struggling
trees, bent and twisted like snakes. On the ground he could
see a whole carpet of creeping brown spruce twigs and
needles, and above them cave-like holes of gaping darkness.

"Look!" he said. "There's a spruce holding a little birch
tree in its arms to protect it."

"Do you think so?" said Little My sinisterly. "I think
she's strangling it. This is just the sort of forest where people
get strangled. I shouldn't be surprised if there's somebody in
there being strangled right now. Like this!"—She threw her
arms round Moomintroll's neck and began to squeeze him.

"Give over!" screamed Moomintroll and shook himself

loose. "Do you really think there's someone in there . . . ?"

"You take me too literally," said Little My with contempt.

"No I don't," exclaimed Moomintroll. "It's only that I can *see* someone sitting in there! It seems so real, but I never know if people are serious or just pulling my leg. Are you being serious? *Is* there really someone there?"

Little My laughed and got up. "Don't be stupid," she said. "So long. I'm off to the point to take a look at that queer old fisherman. He interests me."

After Little My had gone, Moomintroll crept a little closer to the forest and stared in, his heart beating fast. He could hear the waves breaking gently on the beach and the sun was warm on his back.

"Of course there's nobody there," thought Moomintroll, angrily. "She just made it up. I know she's always making things up and getting me to believe them. Next time she does it I'll say: 'Huh! Don't be silly!' A bit superciliously, and in passing, of course. This forest isn't dangerous, it's just scared. Every single tree is bending backwards as though it wanted to pull itself by the roots and run away. You can see it." And still angry, Moomintroll crept right into the thicket.

The sunshine disappeared and it grew cold. The branches tore at his ears and the twigs pricked him, and hollow bits of wood snapped under his paws. There was a smell of cellars and dead plants. And it was quiet, quite silent, and the noise of the sea could no longer be heard. Moomintroll thought he could hear someone breathing and he felt himself choking with panic, shut in and being strangled by the trees. He wanted terribly to get out into the sunshine again, quickly, quickly—and then he thought: "No. If I turn back now, I shall never dare to go in again. Little My has frightened me, that's all. I shall say to her: 'Oh, by the way, there's nothing in the thicket at all. I looked. You were bluffing'!"

Moomintroll sneezed and crept a little further, groping between the trees. Now and again there was a crack and a tree-trunk fell to the ground, a soft, velvet-brown mass of decaying wood. The ground was like elastic and as smooth as silk, and was covered with millions of dead needles.

As he crept farther and farther in, the unpleasant shut-in feeling vanished. He just felt protected and hidden by the chilly darkness; he was a tiny little animal who was hiding and wanted to be left in peace. Suddenly he could hear the sea again and feel the warmth and dazzling brightness of the sun. He had come upon a glade in the middle of the thicket.

It was a very small glade, about as big as two beds placed side by side. Inside it was warm and there were bees buzzing round the flowers. On all sides the forest stood guard. Above his head the birch trees waved to and fro, a thin green roof which the sun could look through. It was complete. Moomintroll had found perfection. Nobody had been here before him; it was all his own.

He sat carefully down in the grass and shut his eyes. To have a really safe hiding-place had always been one of his most serious ambitions, he had always been looking for one, and had found quite a number in the past. But none of them had been as good as this. It was both hidden and open. Only the birds could see him, the ground was warm and he was protected on all sides. He sighed.

Something bit Moomintroll's tail. It stung like mad. He jumped up and he knew at once what it was. Ants. Tiny, vindictive red ants. There were swarms of them in the grass. they were running in all directions—another one bit him in the tail. Moomintroll withdrew slowly, his eyes red with disappointment; he was terribly offended. Naturally, they were living here before he had appeared on the scene. But if one lives in the ground, one just doesn't see anything of what's up above; an ant has no idea of what birds or clouds look like, or for that matter doesn't know anything about the things which are important to a Moomintroll for instance.

There were many kinds of justice. According to one kind, which was a little complicated perhaps, but absolutely fair, the glade belonged to him and not to the ants. "But how can I get them to understand?" he thought. "They could just as easily live somewhere else. Just a little way off, only a few yards. Was there no way of explaining to them? If the worst came to the worst, couldn't one just draw a boundary line and divide the glade?"

They were back again. They had located him and started to attack. Moomintroll fled. He was fleeing from paradise in disgrace, but he was fully determined to return. The place had been waiting for him all his life, perhaps for several

hundred years! It was his because he liked it more than anybody else did. If a million ants all loved it at the same time,
they couldn't feel as strongly as he did. Or so he believed.

*   *   *

"Pappa," said Moomintroll.

But Moominpappa wasn't listening, because just at that
moment he had got the right grip on a big round boulder,
and with a great thud it rolled down the slope. It made two
very clear sparks and left a faint but enchanting smell of
gunpowder behind. Now it was lying at the bottom, just
where it should lie. It was wonderful to roll stones, first
pushing with all one's might, then feeling them beginning to
move, just a little at first—then a little more—and then
giving way and rolling into the sea with a colossal splash,
leaving one standing there trembling with effort and pride.

"Pappa!" shouted Moomintroll.

Moominpappa turned round and waved to his son. "It's
lying just where it should lie!" he exclaimed. "This is going
to be a jetty, a kind of breakwater." He waded into the sea
and with a great deal of puffing and blowing, began to roll
another, even larger boulder along the bottom, with his nose
right under the water. It was much easier to lift and roll
stones under the water. Moominpappa wondered why. But
the great thing was that it made one feel tremendously
strong . . .

"I want to ask you something!" shouted Moomintroll.
"About red ants! It's important!"

Moominpappa lifted his nose out of the water and listened.

"Red ants!" repeated Moomintroll. "Can one talk to
them? Do you think they would understand if I put up a
notice for them? Could they read it?"

"Red ants?" said Moominpappa in amazement. "Of

course they can't read. They wouldn't understand a thing. Now I must find a three-cornered stone to put in between these two large ones. A breakwater has to be strong—it must be built by someone who knows all about the sea . . ." Pappa went on wading, with his nose in the water.

Moomintroll went higher up the beach and stood where he could see Moominmamma crawling about in her garden. She was spreading out seaweed. Her paws and apron were quite brown and she radiated happy concentration.

Moomintroll went up to her and said: "Mamma, just try and imagine a perfectly marvellous spot that you've found and made your very own, only to discover that there are crowds of other people there who don't want to move away. Have they the right to stay put, although they don't understand how beautiful the place is?"

"Yes, of course they have," said Moominmamma, sitting down in the seaweed.

"But what if they would be just as happy in a rubbish-heap?" exclaimed her son.

"Well, then one would have to reason with them," said Moominmamma. "And perhaps give them a hand with the moving. It's very trying to have to move if one has lived in the same place for a long time."

"Oh, bother!" said Moomintroll. "Where's Little My?"

"She's somewhere up at the lighthouse, building some sort of lift," answered Moominmamma.

*   *   *

Little My was hanging perilously out of the open north window as bold as brass. She was knocking a nail into a block of wood on the window-ledge. On the floor there was a whole pile of grey-looking things and the trap-door was open.

"What do you think Pappa will say about this?" Moomintroll asked. "No one's allowed up there. It's his private room."

"There's a loft above his private room," said Little My nonchalantly. "A jolly nice little loft where you can find all sorts of things. Hand me that nail. I'm fed up with climbing up those stairs every time we have to eat, so I'm building a lift. You can haul me up in a basket, or else lower the food down to me. That would be even better."

"How she carries on!" Moomintroll thought. "She does exactly what she feels like doing, and no one opposes her. She just does it."

He said: "By the way, that thicket. There's no one there. No one at all. Possibly a few ants."

"Really," said Littie My. "I can well believe it."

So that was that. She banged a nail right in, whistling between her teeth.

"You'll have to clear up all this mess before Pappa comes back," shouted Moomintroll in between hammer-strokes. But he had a feeling he hadn't made any impression at all. He poked about dejectedly in the pile of old paper, tins, old fishing-nets, woollen gloves and bits of sealskin—and that's how he found the calendar. A large wall-calendar with a wonderful picture of a sea-horse riding on a wave in the moonlight. The moon was dipping into the sea and the sea-horse had long golden hair and very pale, unfathomable eyes. How could anyone paint so beautifully! Moomintroll put the picture on the desk and gazed at it for a long time.

"It's five years out of date," said Little My, jumping down to the floor. "The days are quite different now, and someone's torn them off anyway. Hold the rope, and I'll go down and see if this lift works."

"Wait a minute," said Moomintroll. "There's something

I want to ask you. What does one do to get ants to move?"

"Dig them up, obviously," said Little My.

"No, no," exclaimed Moomintroll. "I mean, to get them to go away."

Little My looked at him. After a while she said: "Ah! I see. So you've found a spot you like in that thicket. And it's full of ants. What will you give me if I get rid of them?"

He felt his nose turn red.

"I'll fix it for you," said Little My calmly. "You can go there and look after a day or two. And you can look after the lift for me instead. I'm off."

Moomintroll stood still, feeling miserable. The secret was out. His hide-out was now just any old place. He looked quickly at the calendar, straight into the sea-horse's eyes. "We're alike, you and I," he thought. "We understand each other, we only care about beautiful things. I shall get my glade, and nothing else matters. But just at the moment I don't want to think about it."

Little My pulled on the rope down below. "Pull me up!" she shouted. "And don't let go! Think of your ants."

The lift worked perfectly. Actually she had never supposed it would do anything else.

*   *   *

Tired but happy, Moominpappa walked home through the heather. Naturally, somewhere in the back of his mind he knew that he would have to try again to make the lamp work, but there were still some hours left before dusk. And he had been rolling big stones, enormous ones, and every time one of them rolled down into the water, Moomin-mamma had turned her head and watched from the garden. Moominpappa decided to go round by the western point.

On the leeward side the fisherman rowed past with his

fishing rods in the bow of his boat. Moominpappa had never
heard that it was possible to get the fish to bite with a rod and
line so late in the year. July was the month for that. But he
wasn't an ordinary fisherman. Perhaps he liked being by
himself. Moominpappa lifted his paw to wave, but didn't.
He wouldn't get an answer anyway.

He climbed up the rock and began to walk into the wind.
Here the rocks were curved and looked like the backs of
enormous animals walking side by side towards the sea.
He had reached the pool before he caught sight of it. The
water in it was calm and dark, and it was oval in shape,
looking like a great big eye. Moominpappa was delighted. A
real lake, a black pool, one of the most mysterious things one
could find! From time to time a little wave found its way in
from the sea. It slipped in over the threshold, shattering the
mirror-like surface of the water for a moment, and then the
pool became calm again, staring blankly up at the sky.

"It's deep down there," thought Moominpappa. "It
must be very deep indeed. This island of mine is a complete
world of its own, it has everything and is just the right size.
How happy I feel! I've got the world in my paw!"

Moominpappa went back to the lighthouse as fast as he
could. He wanted to show them all the black pool before
they found it for themselves.

*   *   *

"What a pity it isn't rainwater," said Moominmamma.

"No, no, it was made by the sea!" said Moominpappa,
gesticulating with his paws. "Great storms have flung the
sea over the island and rolled stones round and round at the
bottom until it has become terribly deep."

"Perhaps there are some fish in it," Moominmamma
suggested.

"Very possibly," said Moominpappa. "But if there are any, they must be gigantic. Imagine a giant pike which has been down there for a hundred years, just getting fatter and angrier the whole time!"

"That really would be something!" said Little My, impressed. "Perhaps I'll throw in a line and find out."

"Angling is not for little girls," said Moominpappa firmly. "No, the black pool is for fathers. And don't go too near the edge! You must realise that it's a very dangerous spot. I shall make very careful investigations, but not just at the moment. There's the jetty to think about, and then I must make an oven for smoking eel and pike weighing more than fourteen pounds. And I must put out the nets before it starts to rain . . ."

"And some sort of guttering for the roof," added Moominmamma. "In a couple of days we shall have no drinking water left."

"Don't worry, my dear," said Moominpappa protectively. "You'll get a gutter all right. Be patient, and I'll do everything."

The family went back towards the lighthouse and Moominpappa continued to talk about the gigantic pike. The wind blew gently through the heather and the setting sun drenched the whole island in warm golden light. But behind them the black pool lay sunk in shadow between the rocks.

*   *   *

Moominmamma had finished clearing up after Little My and the trap door was closed. As soon as he came in, Moominpappa noticed the calendar.

"That's exactly what I need," he said. "Where did you find it? If I'm going to keep any sort of order on this island, I must know what day it is. Today's Tuesday, that I know." Moominpappa picked up a pen and drew a large round circle high up in the margin. That was "The Arrival", and then he made two small crosses underneath for Monday and Tuesday.

"Have you ever seen a sea-horse?" asked Moomintroll. "Are they as beautiful as those in the picture?"

"Possibly," said Moominmamma. "I don't know. They do say that the painters of pictures exaggerate."

Moomintroll nodded thoughtfully. What a pity it was that you couldn't tell from the picture whether the little sea-horse had silver shoes or not.

The sunset filled the room with gold, and in a little while it would turn red. Moominpappa stood in the middle of the room thinking. This was the time he ought to go up and light the lamp, but if he climbed the ladder the others would know exactly what he was doing. And when he came down again they would know he hadn't been able to make the lamp work. Why couldn't they keep out of the house until dusk and leave him in peace to try and light it? Sometimes there was something about family life that Moominpappa didn't like. His family wasn't sensitive enough at times like these, although they'd lived with him for so long.

Moominpappa did exactly what one always does at uncomfortable moments—he went and stood in the window with his back to the room.

The marker for the nets lay on the window-sill. Of course. He had completely forgotten to put out the nets. That was important, very important. Moominpappa felt a great sense of relief. He turned round and said: "We'll put the nets out tonight. They ought to be in the sea before sunset. Actually, we ought to put them out every night now that we're living on an island."

Moomintroll and his father rowed out with the nets.

"We must put them out in an arc from the east point," Moominpappa said. "The west point belongs to the fisherman. It wouldn't be right to start fishing right under his very nose. Now row slowly while I keep an eye on the bottom."

The water began to get deeper in very gentle, sweeping terraces of sand, descending in the water like a broad ceremonial staircase. Moomintroll rowed towards the point over forests of seaweed that got darker and darker.

"Stop!" shouted Moominpappa. "Go back a bit. The bottom's fine just here. We'll lay it out obliquely towards those rocks. Slowly now!"

He threw in the float with its little white pennant and dipped the net into the sea. It glided out slowly with long even movements, drops of water shining in the mesh. The

corks rested on the surface for a moment, and then they saw them sink, like a necklace of beads behind them. It was a very satisfying feeling putting a net out. It was a man's job, something one did for the whole family.

When all three nets were out, Moominpappa spat three times on the marker and dropped it in. It stuck its tail in the air and disappeared straight down in the water. Moominpappa sat down in the stern of the boat.

It was a peaceful evening. The colours were beginning to grow pale and disappear in the dusk, but right over the thicket the sky was still quite red. They pulled the boat up the beach in silence, and then walked home across the island.

When they had got as far as the poplars, they heard a faint wailing coming over the water. Moomintroll stood still.

"I heard that noise yesterday, too," said Moominpappa. "It's a bird, I expect."

Moomintroll looked out across the sea.

"There's something sitting on that rock," he said.

"That's a beacon," said Moominpappa, and walked on.

"There was no beacon there yesterday," thought Moomintroll. "There was nothing there at all." He stood stock-still and waited.

It was moving. Very, very slowly it glided over the rock and was gone. It couldn't be the fisherman. He was short and thin. It was something else.

Moomintroll pulled himself together and continued on his way home. He wouldn't say anything before he was certain. Anyway Moomintroll hoped that he would never know what it was that sat out there wailing every evening.

*   *   *

Moomintroll woke up in the middle of the night. He lay quite still, listening. Someone had called him. But he wasn't quite sure, perhaps he had only dreamed it. The night was just as calm as the evening had been, full of a blue-white light, and the waxing moon was high over the island.

Moomintroll got out of bed as quietly as he could so as not to wake Moominpappa and Moominmamma, and went up to the window, opened it carefully and looked out. Now he could hear the faint sound of the waves breaking on the beach, and see the dark rocks floating forlornly in the sea. Far away a bird called; the island was completely at rest.

No—something was happening down on the beach. The distant fall of hurrying feet, something splashing in the water —something was happening down there. Moomintroll became intensely excited. He was sure that whatever it was concerned him, only him and none of the others. He must go down there and see for himself. Something told him that it was important, and that he must go out into the night and see what was happening down there on the beach. Somebody was calling him and he mustn't be afraid.

When he was by the door he remembered the stairs and hesitated. The winding stairs at night were an awful thought —in the day you could run up them, not giving yourself time to think. Moomintroll went back into the room and took the hurricane lamp off the table. He found the matches on the mantelpiece.

The door closed behind him, and the tower opened up below him like a deep, dark well. He couldn't see it, but he knew it was there. The flame of the hurricane lamp flickered, rose and fell, and then burnt steadily. He put it down and plucked up courage to take a look.

The light had frightened all the shadows, and they fluttered giddily all round him when he lifted the lamp up. So many of them, fantastic shapes flickering up and down the hollow inside of the lighthouse. It was beautiful. The stair-case wound downwards, down, down, down, grey and fragile like the skeleton of some prehistoric animal, and was lost in the darkness at the bottom. With every step he took, the shadows danced on the walls all round him. It was much too beautiful to think of being frightened.

So Moomintroll went down the stairs, step by step, holding the lamp tightly, and reached the muddy floor at the bottom of the lighthouse. The door creaked as usual and it felt very heavy. He stood outside on the rock in the cold, unreal moonlight.

"Isn't life exciting!" Moomintroll thought. "Everything can change all of a sudden, and for no reason at all! The staircase is suddenly quite beautiful, and the glade something I don't want to think about any more."

Breathlessly, he walked over the rock, through the heather, through the little copse of aspens. They were motionless and quiet now, there wasn't a breath of wind. He walked slowly, listening. The beach was quite quiet.

"I've frightened them," Moomintroll thought, and bent down to turn out the lamp. "Whatever it is that comes here at night must be very shy. An island by night can be very scared."

Now the lamp was out, and immediately the island seemed to come much nearer. He could feel it very close to him as it lay there motionless in the moonlight. He wasn't at all frightened, but just sat there listening. There it was; the sound of prancing steps in the sand somewhere behind the aspens. Backwards and forwards they went, down the beach into the water, splashing about and making the foam fly.

It was them. The sea-horses, *his* sea-horses. Now he understood everything. The silver shoe he had found in the sand, the calendar with the moon dipping its feet in the mounting wave, the call he had heard while he was asleep. Moomintroll

stood in the trees and watched the sea-horses dance.

They leapt up and down the beach with their heads high, their hair flying and their tails floating behind them in long glistening waves. They were indescribably beautiful, and they seemed to be aware of it. They danced coquettishly, freely and openly, for themselves, for each other, for the island, for the sea—it seemed to be all the same to them. Sometimes they turned suddenly in the water so that the spray rose high above them, making rainbows in the moonlight. Then they would leap back through their own rainbows, looking up and bowing their heads to emphasise the curve of the neck and the line of the back down to the tail. It was as if they were dancing in front of a mirror.

Now they were standing still, stroking each other, obviously thinking only of one another. Both were wearing grey velvet which looked very warm and soft and which never got wet. It looked as if it was patterned with flowers.

While Moomintroll was watching them, something curious but quite natural happened. He suddenly thought that he, too, was beautiful. He felt relaxed and playful and light-of-heart. He ran down the beach crying: "Look at the moonlight! It's so warm! I feel I could fly!"

The sea-horses shied, reared and sprang away in the moonlight. They dashed past him with their eyes staring and their hair streaming and their hooves beating the ground in panic, but he knew all the time that they were only pretending. He knew that they weren't really frightened and he didn't know whether he ought to clap or try to calm them down. He just felt small, and fat and clumsy again. As they flew past him into the sea he shouted: "You're so beautiful, so beautiful! Don't leave me!" A cloud of spray rose in the air, the last rainbow disappeared and the beach was deserted.

Moomintroll sat down in the sand to wait. He felt sure

they would come back. They were certain to come back if he was only patient enough.

The night passed and the moon went down.

"Perhaps they would like to see a light on the beach, a light to tempt them back here to play," thought Moomintroll. He lit the hurricane lamp and put it in front of him on the sand, staring intently at the dark water. After a while he got up and began to swing the lamp backwards and forwards. It was a signal. He tried to think of only ordinary soothing things and went on swinging the lamp. He was very, very patient.

It began to get cold on the beach, perhaps because it was getting on for morning. The cold floated in from the sea and Moomintroll's paws began to freeze. He shivered and looked up; there was the Groke sitting on the water in front of him.

Her eyes were following the movements of the hurricane lamp, but otherwise she didn't move. But he knew she would come nearer. He didn't want to have anything to do with her. He wanted to go away from the coldness and motionlessness of her, far away from the terrifying loneliness of her. But he couldn't move. He just couldn't.

He stood there swinging the hurricane lamp slower and slower. Neither of them moved and time began to drag. In the end Moomintroll started to walk backwards very slowly. The Groke stayed where she was on her little island of ice. Moomintroll went on walking backwards without taking his eyes off her, up the beach, into the aspens He turned the lamp out.

It was very dark and the moon had gone down behind the island. Was that a shadow moving across the water?—he couldn't be sure. Moomintroll went back to the lighthouse, his head full of things to think about.

The sea was quite calm now, but in among the aspens the leaves whispered with fright. He could smell paraffin strongly, coming from the thicket. But it didn't seem to belong to the island somehow, or to the night.

"I'll think about that tomorrow," said Moomintroll to himself. "I've more important things on my mind now."

The North-Easter

Just before sunrise, the wind got up. It was a vile, stubborn wind, blowing from the east. The family woke at about eight o'clock, and by then the wind was blowing in showers from the east and gusts of rain were sweeping round the lighthouse.

"Now we shall get some water," said Moominmamma. "Thank goodness I found that barrel and cleaned it!" She put some wood on the fire and lit it.

Moomintroll was still in bed. He didn't want to talk to anyone. A wet patch had appeared on the ceiling, and a drop of water was getting larger and larger in the middle of it. Then it fell on to the table and another one started to form immediately.

Little My crept in through the door. "This is no weather for the lift," she said, squeezing the water out of her hair. "The wind's blowing it straight off the lighthouse wall."

They could hear the wind howling round the tower and the door shut with a bang.

"Is coffee ready?" asked Little My. "Weather like this makes me feel ravenous. The sea's swept right into the black pool and the old man's point has become an island! He's blown inside out and is lying under his boat counting raindrops."

"The nets!" said Moominpappa, jumping out of bed. "We've got the nets out." He went to the window but couldn't see a trace of the float. The east wind was blowing in right over the point. It would be a ghastly job pulling them up with the wind blowing from the side. And the rain, too.

"They can stay where they are," decided Moominpappa. "There'll just be more fish in them, that's all. After I've had my breakfast I'll take a turn up above and see if I can get the hang of this gale. It will have blown itself out by this evening, you'll see."

*   *   *

The gale looked just the same from up above. Moominpappa stood looking at the lamp, unscrewed a nut and then screwed it up again, and opened and closed the lamp door. It was useless, he still didn't know how it worked. How utterly thoughtless not to leave proper instructions in a lighthouse like this! Unforgivable, really.

Moominpappa sat on one of the gas cylinders and leant against the wall. Above him the rain was beating on the window-panes, lashing and whipping them as each gust blew past. The green pane was broken. On the floor beneath it a little lake had formed. Moominpappa looked at it absently, and imagined it was a delta with long, winding rivers, and let his eyes wander across the wall. Someone had written something that looked like poetry with a pencil. Moominpappa leant closer and read it:

> Out there on the empty sea,
> Where only the moon appears,
> No sail has been seen to pass
> In four long and dreary years.

"The lighthouse-keeper must have written that," Moominpappa thought. "He thought of it one day when he felt miserable. Imagine lighting the lamp for ships that never go past." Higher up the wall he had been feeling more cheerful, and had written:

> A wind from the east, and old hags' jeers,
> Will both, as a rule, end up in tears.

Moominpappa started to creep round the walls looking for things the lighthouse-keeper had written. There were many notes about the strength of the wind. Apparently the worst storm had been one with a south-westerly wind, force ten. In another place the lighthouse-keeper had written some more verses, but they had been crossed out with heavy black lines. All he could pick out was something about birds.

"I must find out more about him," thought Moominpappa. "As soon as it clears up I must go and find the fisherman. They must have known one another. They lived on the same island. Now I'm going to shut this trap-door. I shan't come up here any more. It's too depressing."

He climbed down the ladder, and said: "It's moving a little towards the north-east. Perhaps it will die down. By the way, we ought to ask that fisherman to coffee some day."

"I bet he doesn't drink coffee," said Little My. "I'm sure he only eats seaweed and raw fish. Perhaps he sucks up plankton through his front teeth."

"What did you say?" exclaimed Moominmamma. "What curious taste he has!"

"He looks as if he didn't eat anything else," added Little

My. "It wouldn't surprise me in the least. But he knows his own mind, and he never asks questions," she said appreciatively.

"Doesn't he tell you anything, either?" asked Moominpappa.

"Not a thing," said Little My. So saying, she climbed up the chimney-piece and curled up against the warm wall to sleep off the rain.

"Anyway, he's our neighbour after all," said Moominmamma vaguely. "One has to have neighbours, I mean." She sighed, and added: "I think the rain's coming in."

"I'll put that right," said Moominpappa. "By and by, when I've got a moment." But he thought: "Perhaps it'll clear up. I don't want to go up there. There's too much there that reminds me of the lighthouse-keeper."

*   *   *

The long, rainy day drew to a close, and towards evening the wind had dropped so much that Moominpappa decided to take up the nets.

"Now you can see I know something about the sea," he said, very pleased with himself. "We shall be back in good time for evening tea, and we shall bring the biggest fish with us. The rest we'll throw back into the sea."

The island was wet everywhere. It seemed to be drooping, and had quite lost its colour in the rain. The water had risen so much that little could be seen of the beach, and the boat was rolling from side to side with its stern in the sea.

"We must pull her right up the beach to the alder bushes," said Moominpappa. "Now you can see what the water can do when autumn comes. If I'd waited till tomorrow morning to take the nets up we shouldn't have had any boat left. You can't be too careful with the sea, you know! I wonder,"

Moominpappa added, "I wonder why the sea rises and falls like this. There must be an explanation . . ."

Moomintroll looked around. The beach had changed completely. The sea looked swollen, it heaved wearily and sulkily and had flung up a heap of seaweed all over the beach. "It's no beach for sea-horses any longer. Imagine if they only like sandy beaches and don't bother to come back again! What if the Groke has scared them away . . ." thought Moomintroll. He threw a timid glance in the direction of the tiny islands offshore, but they had disappeared in the drizzle.

"Watch where you're rowing!" Moominpappa shouted. "Look for the float and mind out for the waves or we'll be driven ashore!"

Moomintroll pulled on his left oar as hard as he could. The *Adventure* swung round to leeward all the time and stuck in the troughs of the waves.

"Row out! Row out!" shouted Moominpappa from the stern. "Turn her round! Backwards! Backwards!" He lay on his stomach over the stern of the boat and tried to reach the float. "No, no, no, no! This way! No, the other way, I mean. That's it. I've got it. Now row straight out!"

Moominpappa caught the net and began to haul it in. The rain was driving in his face and the net felt very heavy.

"We shall never be able to eat all this fish," he thought, a little disconcerted by the thought of such a large catch. "What a job!" he reflected. "But if one has a family, one has a family . . ."

Pulling on the oars like one possessed, Moomintroll saw something dark coming up with the net—it was seaweed! The net was full of seaweed, yards and yards of it!

Moominpappa said nothing. He had stopped trying to take in the net neatly and was lying across the bow of the

boat, pulling the net in any old way with his arms. Armful after armful of thick yellowish-brown seaweed came over the side, but not a single fish. All three nets were the same—nothing but seaweed. Moomintroll turned round and let the boat drift towards the beach while he held the right oar without rowing, and in a few moments the *Adventure* had her nose ashore. The next wave struck her side and she capsized. Moominpappa was suddenly full of life.

"Jump in and pull the prow out," he shouted. "Pull it out and hold on tight!"

Moomintroll stood up to his waist in the water, holding on to the *Adventure* and wave after wave broke over his head. The water was so cold that it was painful. Moominpappa tried to haul the nets ashore, heaving and straining, his hat down over his eyes, and the oars had rolled on to the sand and got tied up with the net and his legs—everything was about as bad as it could be. When they finally got the

Adventure safely up, another sheet of rain drifted in over the sea, and darkness concealed everything. Night was falling.

"Well, we managed that all right," said Moomintroll, looking cautiously at his father.

"Do you think so?" said Moominpappa doubtfully. He stared at the enormous heap of net and seaweed and decided that Moomintroll was right. "Yes, we did," he said. "A battle with the ocean! That's what happens out here, you know."

*   *   *

When Little My heard the story of their adventures, she put the sandwich she was eating on the table in front of her and said: "Well! You two are going to have fun. It'll take three or four days to sort those nets out. That seaweed clings like the very devil. Comes of leaving the net in all day."

"Is that so?" Moominpappa began.

"We've got plenty of time," said Moominmamma quickly. "It might be quite a nice job if the weather's good . . ."

"The fisherman can *eat* them clean," suggested Little My. "He likes seaweed."

Moominpappa felt quite deflated. This seaweed had come right after that wretched business of the lamp, it wasn't fair. One toiled and toiled and nothing worked. Things just seemed to slip through one's fingers. Moominpappa's thoughts started to wander, and he stirred and stirred with his spoon in his cup although the sugar had melted long ago. In the centre of the table stood the smallest saucepan. At intervals a drop fell from the ceiling with a plop. Moomintroll sat staring at the calendar, listlessly making knots in his tail.

"Let's light the lamp!" said Moominmamma cheerfully. "It's stormy tonight, so we can hang it in the window!"

"No, no! Not in the window," shouted Moomintroll, jumping up.

Moominmamma sighed. It was exactly what she was afraid of. The rainy weather was making them behave just as strangely as if they were kept in by the rain on a trip. And there would be lots of rainy days here. There back home there had always been plenty to do indoors, but here . . . Moominmamma got up and went over to the desk and opened the top drawer.

"I went through this today," she said. "It was almost empty. And you can't imagine what I found! A puzzle. There are at least a thousand small pieces here, and no one can tell what it's supposed to be until you put it together. What fun it will be, don't you think?"

She poured the bits on to the table among the tea-cups in an enormous heap. The family stared at it with disapproval.

Moomintroll turned one of the pieces over. It was quite black. As black as the Groke. Or the shadows in the thicket —or the pupils of the sea-horses' eyes. Or a million other things. It might be just anything. You wouldn't know where it fitted in until the whole puzzle was almost finished.

*   *   *

That night the Groke was singing out on the sea. No one had come down to the beach with a lamp. She had waited and waited and no one had come.

She started softly, but gradually her song of loneliness had got louder and louder. It was no longer just sad, it was defiant too. "There's no other Groke, I'm the only one. I'm the coldest thing that ever was. I am never, never warm."

"It's seals," murmured Moominpappa into his pillow.

Moomintroll pulled the blanket over his head. He knew that the Groke was sitting waiting for the lantern. But he wasn't going to let it give him a bad conscience. She could howl as much as she wanted, he didn't care. He didn't care a scrap. And besides, Moominmamma had said that they were using too much paraffin. So that was that.

*   *   *

The days passed, and the water rose as the stubborn east wind continued. The waves swept round the island in a continuous, hypnotic roar. The fisherman's little house was completely cut off, but according to Little My, he was jolly glad to be left in peace. It had stopped raining, and the family had gone down to the beach to look around.

"What masses of seaweed!" exclaimed Moominmamma, delighted to see it. "Now I can make a much larger garden!" She went over the rock and stopped suddenly. The garden had disappeared, completely and utterly vanished. The sea had washed it away.

"Well, it was too near the sea, of course," Moominmamma thought. She was quite crestfallen. "I must carry the seaweed much higher up and start a new one . . ."

She gazed over the flooded beach where the waves were

breaking in a hissing white semicircle. They came right up to
the boat, lying pressed against the alder bushes, striking her
in the stern so that she leapt up in indignation. Moominpappa was standing right out in the water, looking for his
breakwater. He went this way and that, and waded in up to
his waist. He turned round and shouted something.

"What's he saying?" Moominmamma asked.

"It's gone," said Moomintroll. "All the stones have rolled
away."

This was serious. Moominmamma hurried over the wet
sand and out into the water to show that she was sympathetic.
It was better than saying anything at a moment like this.

Moominmamma and Moominpappa stood side by side in
the water getting cold. She thought: "This sea of his *is*
unkind . . ."

"Come, let's go ashore," said Moominpappa absent-
mindedly. "Perhaps those stones weren't as big as I thought
they were."

They left the whole lot behind, and went past the boat
into the aspens, where Moominpappa stopped and said:
"It's no good trying to make a path here. I've tried. These
wretched stones are much too big. The lighthouse-keeper
would have made one long ago if it had been possible, and a
jetty too."

"Perhaps one shouldn't try to change things so much on
this island," said Moominmamma. "Just leave it as it is.
Back home it was easier somehow . . . But I'm going to try
and make a new garden, higher up."

Moominpappa said nothing.

"And there's so much to do in the lighthouse," Moominmamma went on. "One could make lots of little shelves, and
nice furniture! Couldn't one? And mend that awful staircase . . . and the roof . . ."

"I don't want to mend anything," thought Moominpappa. "I don't want to pick seaweed . . . I want to build big
things, strong things, I want to so terribly much . . . But I
don't know . . . It's so very difficult being a father!"

They went towards the lighthouse, and Moomintroll saw
them disappearing up the slope with their tails drooping.

Above the lighthouse-rock he could see a broken rainbow
with all its transparent colours. While he was looking at it,
Moomintroll noticed that the colours were getting fainter,
and he knew at once that it was very important for him to
get to his glade before it disappeared altogether. He rushed
to the thicket, threw himself on his tummy and crawled in.

The glade was his very own, and it was just as beautiful in
cloudy weather. He could see a spider's web between the
branches, all silver with drops of water. Although the wind
was blowing outside, it was quite calm in here. And no ants.
Not a single one.

But perhaps they were just hiding from the rain. Moomintroll started to dig up the turf impatiently with both paws.
There it was again—the smell of paraffin. And there they
were, masses of them, but all dead every one. They were all
shrivelled up. Horror of horrors! A terrible massacre had
taken place, and not a single ant had survived! They were
drenched in paraffin.

Moomintroll got up, and all of a sudden it hit him: "It's
all my fault. I should have known. Little My isn't the sort of
person who talks to people and tries to persuade them. She
acts on the spur of the moment, or nothing at all. What shall
I do? What shall I do?"

Moomintroll sat in his very own glade—his for ever and
ever—swaying backwards and forwards with the smell of
paraffin creeping all over him. It stuck to him all the way
home, and he was sure he would never get rid of it.

*   *   *

"But ants are like mosquitoes," said Little My. "It's a good thing to get rid of them! Anyway, you knew exactly what I was going to do to them! All you hoped was that I shouldn't tell you about it. You're awfully good at deceiving yourself!"

There was no answer to that.

That evening Little My caught sight of Moomintroll creeping through the heather in an obvious attempt to make himself invisible. Naturally, she followed him, and saw him spreading sugar round the edge of the spruce forest. Then he disappeared again into the thicket with a tin.

"Huh!" thought Little My. "Now he's trying to ease his conscience. I *could* tell him that ants don't eat sugar, and that it'll melt anyway because the ground's wet. And that any ant that I didn't catch is completely indifferent to the whole thing, and is in no need of consolation. But I can't be bothered."

*   *   *

Then there were two days when Moominmamma and Moomintroll did nothing but pick seaweed out of the nets.

*   *   *

Then it started to rain again. The wet patch on the ceiling got bigger and bigger. The drops fell "plip, plip, plip" into the little saucepan, and "plop, plop, plop" into the big one. Up in the lamp-room Moominpappa sat contemplating the broken window with great aversion. The more he looked at the wretched window and the more he thought about it, the emptier his mind became. It should be nailed up from the outside, or tightened from the inside with sacking and glue. That's what Moominmamma had suggested.

Moominpappa felt more and more tired, and finally lay on the floor. The green window-pane became a beautiful emerald. He began to feel better, and after a while he was struck by an idea, all his own. "If I was to cut a good wide strip of sacking, and then spread the glue on it, and then break the green glass into lots and lots of emeralds and then press them into the glue . . ." Moominpappa sat up. "What an interesting idea!" he thought.

"In between the emeralds I could throw fine white sand before the glue is too dry. No, perhaps rice instead. That's it —I could work in tiny white grains of rice, like pearls, thousands and thousands of them."

Moominpappa got up and took a hammer to the broken window. He started to prise it away very carefully. A large piece crashed to the floor and splintered. He selected a pawful of little pieces and with endless patience began to hammer the fragments into beautiful even pieces.

*   *   *

Moominpappa came down through the trap-door in the afternoon when the belt was ready.

"I tried it on," he said. "And then I took quite a bit off. It should be just right for you."

Moominmamma put it over her head and it slipped down to her waist, just where it should be.

"It can't be true!" said Moominmamma. "It's the most beautiful thing I've ever been given!"

She was so happy that she suddenly felt very serious.

"We couldn't understand why you wanted rice!" exclaimed Moomintroll. "It swells when its wet . . . so we thought you were using it to tighten the window in some way . . ."

"It's fantastic," said Little My with reluctant admiration.

"I can hardly believe it." She put the wash-basin in a different place so that the drops falling from the ceiling didn't say plip or plop but plup, and added: "Well, that's goodbye to the rice pudding!"

"I have got rather a large waist," said Moominmamma reproachfully. "We can eat gruel just as well."

This suggestion was met by complete silence. Moominpappa could hear the drops falling from the ceiling, making a sort of melody with three notes instead of two, specially written for him. He didn't like it.

"Dearest, if I had to choose between a jewel and rice pudding," Moominmamma began, but Moominpappa interrupted her saying, "How much of the food is eaten?"

"Rather a lot," said Moominmamma anxiously. "You know what sea air is like . . ."

"Is there anything left?" Moominpappa went on.

Moominmamma made a vague gesture which seemed to suggest that there wasn't much left except porridge, but that it wasn't so important after all.

Then Moominpappa did the only possible thing that he could do in such a situation—he took his fishing-rod, put on the lighthouse-keeper's hat, and in proud silence selected his most beautiful trolling spoon.

"I'm going fishing for a while," he said calmly. "It's just the right weather for pike."

      *   *   *

The north-easter had blown itself out, but the water was still very high. It was drizzling, and the rock and the water were the same colour, a grey nothingness and very lonely.

Moominpappa fished for an hour in the black pool. He didn't get a single bite. "One shouldn't talk about pike till one's got a catch," he thought.

Like most fathers of a certain kind Moominpappa liked fishing. He had got his fishing-rod on his birthday a couple of years before and it was a very fine one. But sometimes it stood in its corner in a slightly unpleasant way, as though reminding him that it was for catching fish.

Moominpappa stood looking down into the black water of the pool, and the pool stared back at him with its great eye. He drew in his line and put his pipe in his hat. Then he walked over to the leeward side of the island.

There might be some pike there, little ones perhaps, but something to take home with him anyway.

Just off-shore sat the fisherman fishing in his boat.

"Is this a good place to fish?" Moominpappa asked.

"No," said the fisherman.

Pappa sat on the rock and tried to think of something to say. He had never met anyone so difficult to talk to. It all seemed so clumsy and awkward.

"I expect it's a little lonely here in winter," he ventured, but of course he got no answer. He tried once more.

"But you used to be two here, of course. What was the lighthouse-keeper like?"

The fisherman muttered something and shifted a trifle uneasily on his seat.

"Was he talkative? Did he say much about himself?"

"Everybody does," said the fisherman suddenly. "They talk about themselves. He talked about himself always. But maybe I didn't listen to him. I forget."

"How did he come to leave here?" Moominpappa asked. "Did the lighthouse go out before he left or after he'd gone?"

The fisherman shrugged his shoulders and drew in his line. The hook was empty. "I've forgotten," he said.

In desperation Moominpappa made yet another attempt. "But what did he do all day? Did he build something? Did he put out any nets?"

The fisherman threw out his line with a beautiful, slow movement, making a perfect circle on the surface of the water which spread out gently and disappeared. He turned and looked out to sea.

Moominpappa rose and walked on. Somehow it was a relief to feel as angry as he did. He cast his line out quite a way, without bothering to see whether he was observing that tactful distance which one gentleman ought to observe when he's fishing close to another. He got a bite immediately.

He pulled in a perch weighing a pound. He made a great deal of fuss about it, puffing and blowing and splashing about, and slapping the perch on the rock, just to annoy the fisherman as much as possible. He looked at the grey figure sitting motionless and staring out to sea.

"This pike's probably about five pounds!" he said loudly, hiding the perch behind his back. "It'll be quite a job to smoke!"

The fisherman didn't move an inch.

"That'll teach him!" Moominpappa muttered. "Think of that poor lighthouse-keeper talking and talking about himself and that—that little shrimp not listening." He walked up to the lighthouse with the perch firmly in his paw.

Little My was sitting on the steps, singing one of her monotonous wet-weather songs.

"Hallo," said Moominpappa. "I'm angry."

"Good!" said Little My with approval. "You look as though you'd made a proper enemy of someone. It always helps."

Moominpappa flung the perch on the steps. "Where is she?" he asked.

"Pottering about in that garden of hers," answered Little My. "I'll give her the fish."

Moominpappa nodded and went off towards the western end of the island. "I'll fish right under that man's nose! I'll catch every blessed fish there is. I'll show them . . ."

*   *   *

The ragged nets hung under the staircase in the lighthouse and were easily forgotten. Moominmamma didn't mention small shelves or furniture any more, and the wet patch on the ceiling got bigger and bigger every time it rained. The trap-door remained shut.

Moominpappa didn't bother about anything except fishing. He was out with his line all day and only came home to eat. He left very early in the morning and wouldn't let anyone go with him. He didn't try to provoke the fisherman any more; it's not much fun trying to provoke anybody as small as he was and who refuses to get angry. He had only one very determined thought in his head: getting food for the family. He always placed his catch on the lighthouse steps.

If he caught sizeable fish, he took them down to the beach and smoked them. He sat in front of the stove in the wind, slowly putting twig after twig on the fire to keep it burning evenly. He packed it down carefully with sand and pebbles, he collected juniper twigs and cut chips of alder so that the fish should be done in just the right way. The others didn't see very much of him.

Towards the evening he would take a turn at the black pool, but he never got a bite there.

When they sat round in the evening drinking their tea, he talked about nothing but fish and fishing. He didn't boast in his usual pleasant way. He gave long lectures which Moominmamma listened to in embarrassed surprise, not learning particularly much about anglers and angling.

"He's not playing at it—he's serious," Moominmamma thought. "I've put salt fish in all the jars and containers we possess, and still he goes on fishing. Of course it's grand to have so much food, but somehow it was jollier when we didn't have so much. I think it's the sea that's upset him and made him like this."

Moominmamma wore the emerald belt every day just to show Moominpappa how much she liked it, although of course it was really something dressy which she should only have worn on Sundays. And it was a little tiresome the way the bits of glass got caught in absolutely everything, and unless one moved very carefully the rice kept falling out.

Moominmamma's new garden was ready, a shining circle of seaweed below the lighthouse-rock. She had put small round pebbles all the way round it as the sea refused to provide her with any shells. In the centre was the rose she had brought with her from home, standing in the soil it had come in. A rose was just about to come out, but it seemed doubtful whether to or not. This was natural, of course, as it was already well into September.

Moominmamma often dreamed about all the flowers she would plant when spring came again. She drew them all on the sill of the north window. Every time she sat looking at the sea out of the window, she drew a flower absent-mindedly, with her thoughts on something entirely different. Sometimes she was surprised by her own flowers, they seemed to have grown all by themselves but that only made them the more beautiful.

The seat by the window seemed lonely now that there were no swallows outside. They had flown south on a windy, drizzly day when nobody was looking. The island was now strangely silent; Moominmamma had grown accustomed to their screeching and ceaseless chatter under the eaves. Now only the gulls that swept past her window with yellow eyes that didn't move, and sometimes the cries of cranes flying south—a long way south.

It wasn't actually so curious that neither Moominmamma nor Moominpappa noticed what Moomintroll was doing as they were always thinking of other things. They knew nothing about the thicket or the glade, they were unaware that every night after the moon had risen Moomintroll went down to the beach with the hurricane lamp.

What Little My saw and thought, no one knew. Most of the time she followed the fisherman around, but they hardly ever spoke to one another. They merely tolerated each other, slightly amused and mutually independent. They didn't bother to try to understand one another or to make any impression on one another; that is also a way of enjoying oneself.

This is how things stood on the island the autumn night when the sea-horses came back.

*   *   *

There was nothing new in going down to the beach with the hurricane lamp. Moomintroll had got used to the Groke; actually she was more of a nuisance than a danger. He didn't

really know whether he went down to the beach for her sake
or just in the hope that the sea-horses would come back. It
was just that he woke up as soon as the moon rose and simply
had to get up.

The Groke was always there. She stood a little way out on
the water watching the movements of the lamp with her
eyes. When he put the lamp out, she floated off into the
darkness again without making a sound, and then Moomintroll went home.

But each night she came a little nearer. Tonight there she was sitting on the sand, waiting.

Moomintroll stopped by the alder bushes and put the lamp down on the ground. The Groke had broken the ritual by coming up the beach; it was wrong of her. She had nothing to do with the island, she was a danger to everything growing there, everything that was alive.

They stood in silence facing each other as they usually did. The Groke took her eyes off the lamp and stared at Moomintroll. She had never done that before. She had such cold eyes, and they looked so anxious. The beach was full of fleeting shadows as the moon went behind the clouds, then appeared again.

Then the sea-horses came galloping along from the point. They didn't take the slightest notice of the Groke; they chased each other in the moonlight, throwing up rainbows and jumping through them. Moomintroll noticed that one of them had lost a shoe. She'd got only three. She really *had* flowers on her coat, some sort of daisy, a little smaller on her neck and legs. Or perhaps they were water-lilies, which were perhaps more poetic. She ran right over the hurricane lamp, and it fell over in the sand.

"You're spoiling my moonlight! My moonlight!" cried the little sea-horse.

"I'm sorry," said Moomintroll, immediately putting the lamp out as fast as he could.

"I found your shoe . . ."

The sea-horse stopped and put her head on one side.

"But I'm afraid I gave it to my mother," Moomintroll continued.

The moon disappeared, the galloping hooves came back and Moomintroll could hear the sea-horses laughing.

"Did you hear that? Did you hear that?" they shouted to

each other. "He's given it to his mother! To his mother! To his mother!"

They galloped towards him, brushing up against him. Their manes brushed his face like soft silky grass.

"I can ask for it back! I can go and fetch it!" he called into the darkness.

The moon came out again. He saw the sea-horses go into the sea side by side, their hair floating behind them. They were exactly alike. One of them turned her head and called distantly: "Another night . . ."

Moomintroll sat down on the sand. She had spoken to him. She had promised to come back. There would be moonlight for many nights to come if only it wasn't cloudy. And he would make sure not to light the hurricane lamp.

He suddenly realised that his tail was freezing. He was sitting on the very spot where the Groke had sat.

*   *   *

The following night he went down to the beach without taking the hurricane lamp with him. The moon was on the wane now, the time when the sea-horses would soon go and play somewhere else. This he knew, and felt it instinctively.

Moomintroll had the silver horseshoe with him. It hadn't been an easy matter getting it back. He had blushed and behaved terribly awkwardly. Moominmamma had taken the horseshoe off its nail without asking why he wanted it.

"I've rubbed it with silver-polish," she had said. "Look how nicely it's come up!"

No more than that, and in quite an ordinary voice, too.

Moomintroll had muttered something about giving her something to replace it and taken himself off with his tail between his legs. He *couldn't* explain about the sea-horse, he just couldn't. If only he could find some shells. She would

certainly like to have shells rather than a horseshoe. It would be a simple matter for the sea-horse to bring up a few of the largest and most beautiful from the bottom of the sea. That is, of course, if sea-horses cared about other people's mothers. Perhaps it would be better not to ask.

She didn't come.

The moon went down and no sea-horses came at all. Of course she had said "another night" and not "tomorrow night". Another night could be any night. Moomintroll sat and played with the sand and he was very sleepy.

And of course the Groke came. She came over the water in her cloud of cold like somebody's bad conscience, and crept up the beach.

Moomintroll suddenly became incredibly angry.

He backed up to the alder bushes and shouted: "I've no lamp for you! I'm not going to light it for you any more! You shouldn't come here, this island belongs to my father!" He walked away from her backwards, turned and started to run away. The aspens round him trembled and rustled as if there was going to be a storm. They knew that the Groke was on the island.

When he was back in his bed, he heard her howling, and

it seemed much closer than before. "I hope she doesn't come in here," he thought. "As long as the others don't know she's there. She carries on like a fog-horn . . . I know somebody who'll say I'm being stupid, and that's the worst thing of all."

                *   *   *

At the edge of the thicket Little My lay listening under a low-lying branch. She pulled the moss tightly round her and whistled thoughtfully. "Now he's got himself into a nice mess. That's what happens if you start making a fuss of the Groke and imagine you can be friends with a sea-horse."

Then she suddenly remembered the ants and laughed heartily and loudly to herself.

The Fog

Actually, Moominmamma hadn't said anything terrible and certainly nothing that should have made Moominpappa feel annoyed. Nevertheless Moominpappa couldn't for the life of him remember what she had said. It was something about the family having quite enough fish.

It had started by her not admiring the pike enough. They hadn't got any scales, but anyone could see that it was a pike of over six pounds, well—five anyway. When one catches one perch after the other just because one wants to provide for one's family, it's quite an event to catch a pike. And then she had made that remark about having too much fish.

She had been sitting as usual by the window, drawing flowers on the window-sill. It was quite full of flowers all over. Suddenly Moominmamma had said, not looking at anyone in particular, that she just didn't know what to do with all the fish he caught. Or was it that they hadn't any more jars to put them in? Or perhaps it was something about it being nice to have porridge for a change. Something like that anyway.

Moominpappa had put his fishing-rod in the corner and gone out for a walk along the edge of the water, but not near the fisherman's point.

It was a cloudy and completely calm day. You could hardly see the surface of the water heaving in a slow swell after the east wind, and it was as grey as the sky and looked like silk. Some ducks were flying close to the water, very quickly and obviously going about their own business. Moominpappa walked with one paw on the rock and the other in the water, dragging his tail in the sea. The lighthouse-keeper's hat was pulled down over his nose and he was wondering whether there would be a storm or not. A real storm. One would have to rush round saving things and making sure that the family wasn't swept away. Then climb the lighthouse tower and see how strong the wind was . . . come down again and say: "The wind's force thirteen. We must keep quite calm. There's nothing to get worked up about . . ."

Little My was catching sticklebacks.

"Why aren't you fishing?" she asked.

"I've given up fishing," Moominpappa answered.

"That must be a relief for you," Little My remarked. "You must have found it an awful bore after a while."

"You're quite right!" said Moominpappa surprised. "It did become terribly boring. Why didn't I notice it myself?"

He went and sat on the lighthouse-keeper's little ledge and thought: "I must do something different, something new. Something tremendous."

But he didn't know what it was he wanted to do. He was quite bewildered and confused. It reminded him of the time long ago when the Gafsan's daughter had pulled the mat from under his feet. Or like sitting in the air next to a chair but not on it. No it wasn't like that either. It was as if he had been taken in by something.

As he sat there looking at the silky-grey surface of the sea that seemed to refuse to work itself up into a storm, the feeling of being taken in by somebody or something got stronger and stronger. "Just you wait," he muttered to himself,

"I'll find out, I'll get to the bottom of this . . ." He didn't know whether he meant the sea, the island or the black pool. Perhaps he meant the lighthouse or the lighthouse-keeper. In any case it sounded very menacing. He shook his perplexed head and went and sat by the black pool. There he continued to think, his nose in his paws. From time to time the breakers washed in over the threshold and disappeared in the black, mirror-like water.

"This is where storms have washed in for hundreds of years," he thought. "Cork floats and pieces of bark and small sticks have been carried in by the waves and then carried out again, it must have happened like that many, many times . . . Until one day . . ." Moominpappa lifted his nose and an extraordinary idea suddenly occurred to him.

"Imagine if suddenly one day something really big and heavy, something from a wreck, was swept in and sank there and stayed at the bottom for ever and ever!"

Moominpappa got up. Treasure trove, perhaps. A case of contraband whisky. The skeleton of a pirate. Anything! The whole pool might be full of the most incredible things!

He felt tremendously happy. He immediately became full of life. Something seemed to wake up inside him as if a steel spring had suddenly been released like a jack-in-the-box, setting him in motion. He rushed home, flew up the stairs two at a time, pushed open the door and shouted: "I've got an idea!"

"You haven't!" exclaimed Moominmamma, who was standing by the stove. "Is it a good one?"

"Of course it is," Moominpappa answered. "It's a grand idea. Come and sit down and I'll tell you all about it."

Moominmamma sat down on one of the empty boxes and Moominpappa began to tell her all about his idea. When he had finished Moominmamma said: "Why, it's incredible!

Only you could have thought of something like that. There might be just anything down there!"

"Exactly," said Moominpappa. "Just anything." They looked at each other and laughed. "When are you going to start looking?" Moominmamma asked.

"Immediately, of course," said Moominpappa. "I shall drag the pool thoroughly. But first I must find out how deep it is. We must try and get the boat into the pool. You see, if I try to haul everything up the cliff face it might fall down again. And it's very important to reach the middle of the pool. Obviously the best things are there."

"Don't you want any help?" Moominmamma asked.

"Oh no," said Moominpappa. "This is a job that I must do. I must find a plumb-line . . ." He went up the ladder, through the trap-door and into the lamp-room without giving the lamp a single thought and higher up to the loft above. After a while he came down again with a rope and asked: "Have you got anything I can use as a weight?" Moominmamma rushed to the stove and gave him the iron.

"Thanks," Moominpappa said, disappearing through the door. She heard him running down the stairs two at a time. Then all was quiet again.

Moominmamma sat down at the table and laughed. "How wonderful," she said. "What a relief!"

*   *   *

Moomintroll lay in his glade watching the birch leaves waving above him. They were turning yellow and looked more beautiful than ever.

He had made three separate entrances to his house: the front door, the kitchen door and an emergency door if he had to escape suddenly. He had patiently filled in the green walls of the house with plaited branches and he had made the glade his very own by doing it up for himself.

Moomintroll didn't think about the ants any more. They had become a part of the ground beneath him. The smell of paraffin had disappeared, and new flowers would grow where the old ones had died. He supposed that round the thicket there were thousands of happy little red ants enjoying the sugar. Everything was just right.

No, he was thinking about the sea-horses. Something had happened to him. He had become quite a different troll, with quite different thoughts. He liked being all by himself. It was much more exciting to play games in his imagination, to have thoughts about himself and the sea-horses, of the moonlight, and the Groke's shadow was always in his thoughts, too. He knew she was sitting somewhere out there all the time. She howled at night, but it didn't matter. Or so he thought.

He had collected all sorts of presents for the sea-horses. Beautiful pebbles and bits of glass, rubbed smooth by the sea until they looked like jewels. And some smooth copper weights which he had taken from the lighthouse-keeper's drawer. He imagined what the sea-horse would say when he gave them to her, he had worked out all sorts of clever and poetic things to say to her.

He was waiting for the moon to come back.

*   *   *

Moominmamma had put everything they had brought with them from home in order long ago. There was no need for her to do much cleaning. Out here there was hardly any dust at all, and in any case one shouldn't make too much fuss about cleaning. Preparing meals was easy, too, provided one did it in the most light-hearted way possible. And so the days came to seem long in quite the wrong way.

And she didn't want to do the puzzle because it reminded her that she was so much alone.

One day she started to collect wood. She picked up every little stick she found, until the beach was clean of everything the sea had washed up. Gradually she had gathered together a large pile of logs and bits of plank. The nice thing about it was that she had tidied up the island at the same time; it made her feel as though the island was like a garden that could be cleaned up and made to look beautiful.

She carried everything herself to a place she had chosen to the leeward of the lighthouse-rock. There she had nailed together a horse for sawing the wood on. It was a little crooked, but it worked all right if she held the right side with her paw.

Moominmamma sawed and sawed in the mild, overcast weather. She measured every bit so that they were all exactly the same size and arranged them neatly in a half-circle round her. The wall of wood round her grew higher and higher, until she stood there sawing in an enclosed space all her own that gave her a lovely feeling of security. She

stacked the dry sticks by the stove, but she didn't have the
heart to tackle the really big logs. But she had never been
particularly good at wielding an axe.

Close by the place where she piled the wood there was
growing a little mountain-ash, to which she became very
attached. It was covered with red berries, lots and lots of
them for such a little tree. She collected the best bits of wood
under this tree. Moominmamma knew a lot about trees; she
knew what oak was and jacaranda; she recognised balsam
and Oregon pine and mahogany. They all had a different
smell, felt different to the touch. They had all reached her
after a long, long journey.

"Jacaranda and palisanda," murmured Moominmamma
to herself, deeply satisfied, and went on sawing.

The others had got used to Moominmamma sawing, and
they could see less and less of her behind her wall of wood. In
the beginning Moominpappa had been very upset and had
wanted to collect the wood himself. But Moominmamma had
got angry and said: "This job's mine. I want to play too!"
And she went on sawing and sawing, going round the island
every morning, looking for fresh pieces of wood.

One grey, absolutely calm, morning Moominmamma
found a shell on the beach. It was a big conch shell, pink
inside and pale brown with dark spots outside.

Moominmamma was both pleased and surprised. It was
lying high up on the beach although the water hadn't come
so far for a week. A little farther off she found a white one,
the kind one puts round borders in a garden. As a matter of
fact, there were shells all over the beach, large ones and small
ones, and the most remarkable thing was that on one of them
she read "A present from the seaside", written on it in tiny
red letters.

Moominmamma was even more surprised, and began to

collect them all in her apron. Then she went to show them to Moominpappa, who was busy dragging the black pool.

He lay with his nose over the side of the boat, looking very small from the top of the cliff. The boat was drifting, with the oars trailing in the water.

"Come and look!" Moominmamma called.

Moominpappa rowed over to the side of the pool.

"Look! Real shells!" Moominmamma said. "I found them high up on the beach, and there were none there yesterday at all!"

"That's very strange," said Moominpappa, knocking his pipe out on the rock. "One of the mysteries of the sea. Sometimes I'm quite fascinated when I think of the way the sea behaves in such a mysterious way. You say they were lying high up on the beach and weren't there yesterday? Well, that must mean that the sea can rise a whole yard in a few hours and then fall again, although we don't have the tides here that they do further south. Very interesting, very interesting indeed! And the inscription on this one—well, it opens up limitless possibilities." He looked at Moominmamma very seriously. "You know, it's things like this I must get really worked out and perhaps write a book about. Everything to do with the sea, and I mean the real sea. I must find out all I can about the sea. Jetties and paths and fishing are for small-minded people who don't care about the really big things." He repeated very solemnly, "the really big things", it sounded most impressive. "It's this black pool which has made me think of all this."

"Is it deep?" Moominmamma asked, opening her eyes wide.

"Very deep," Moominpappa said. "The plumb-line hardly reaches to the bottom. Yesterday I hauled up this metal canister, which proves my theories are right."

Moominmamma nodded. After a while she said: "Well, perhaps I'll go and put these shells in the garden."

Moominpappa didn't answer. He was lost in profound thoughts and speculation.

*   *   *

At about the same time, Moomintroll was burning a box which had been stripped of all its shells, in Moominmamma's stove. It wasn't worth keeping now that he had taken all the shells off. He had found it in the bottom drawer of the desk, the one Moominmamma hadn't wanted to touch because it obviously contained the lighthouse-keeper's most personal belongings.

*   *   *

The metal canister was rusty and broken, and had probably never had anything more interesting than turpentine or oil in it. But it was a proof. The black pool was the place where the sea hid things, things it wanted to keep secret. Moominpappa was convinced with a desperate certainty that at the bottom all these secrets were waiting for him. And there might be just anything down there. He thought that if he could only get everything up he would understand the sea, everything would fall into place. He felt he would fit in, too.

So Moominpappa went on dragging with dogged determination in the middle of the pool and lowering the plumb-line again and again. He had called the centre of the pool "the unfathomable depths". "The Unfathomable Depths", he whispered to himself, and felt his spine tingle with the magic of the phrase.

Most of the time, the line stopped at different depths. But it could also go down and down without touching the bottom

however hard he tried to make it reach. The whole boat was full of tangled lines: the washing line, fishing lines, the anchor rope, and every little bit of rope he had been able to lay his paws on, and all really meant to be used for an entirely different purpose, but then that's what always happens with rope.

Moominpappa had worked out a theory that the pool was really a hole leading down to the centre of the earth, it was the crater of an extinct volcano. Finally, he started to write his speculations in an old exercise-book he had found in the loft. Some of the pages of this exercise-book were full of the lighthouse-keeper's notes, small words with long spaces in between them, looking as if a spider had crawled over the paper.

"Libra is in the ascendant, the moon has entered the seventh house," Moominpappa read, "Saturn is in conjunction with Mars." Perhaps the lighthouse-keeper had had visitors on the island after all. That had certainly cheered him up. The rest of it was mostly figures which he didn't understand at all. He turned the book round and started writing at the other end. Most of the time he drew plans of the black pool, some in section and some bird's-eye view,

and became completely absorbed in complicated calculations and explanations of perspective.

Moominpappa didn't talk so much about his investigations any more. By and by he stopped dragging. Instead, he sat on the lighthouse-keeper's ledge just thinking. Sometimes he made some notes about the pool or the sea in the exercise-book.

He might write: "sea-currents are strange and wonderful things to which no one has devoted proper attention", or "the movement of waves is something that will always amaze us" . . . and then he would drop the exercise-book and lose himself in an endless perspective of profound thoughts.

Fog was stealing over the island. It had crept in over the sea without anybody realising it was coming. All of a sudden everything was wrapped in pale-grey mist, and the lighthouse-keeper's ledge seemed to be floating, lonely and deserted, in a woolly void.

Moominpappa liked hiding himself in the fog. He slept a little—until a gull screamed and he woke up with a start. He got up and went on strolling round the island, brooding helplessly over currents and winds, the origin of the rain and of storms, and deep holes in the bottom of the sea that no one could fathom.

Moominmamma saw him emerging from the fog and disappearing again, his nose resting on his stomach, and lost in thought. "He's collecting material," she thought. "Or so he said. Perhaps his exercise-book is full of material. It will be a relief when he's finished!"

She counted out five sweets and put them on a saucer. Then she went and put them on the ledge in the cliff to cheer him up.

*   *   *

Moomintroll lay in the undergrowth looking intently down into a little pool. He dipped the horseshoe in the clear, brown water and watched it turn gold. He could see branches and blades of grass reflected in the water; a very small, upside-down landscape. The twigs stood out very clearly against the fog, and even the tiniest little creature running up and down could be seen.

Moomintroll felt a desperate need to talk to someone about the sea-horse. Just to describe what she looked like. Or just to talk about sea-horses in general.

Now there were two little creepy-crawlies on the same twig. He touched the surface of the water and the miniature landscape vanished. He got up and strolled towards the thicket. Right on the edge of it there was a small beaten track in the moss. "This is probably where Little My lives," he thought. He could hear a rustling sound. She was at home.

Moomintroll took a step forward. The dangerous desire to confide in someone was like a lump sticking in his throat. He bent down and crept in under the branches. There she sat, rolled up like a tiny ball.

"You're in, I see," he said rather stupidly. He sat down in the moss and stared at her.

"What are you holding in your paw?" Little My asked.

"Nothing," answered Moomintroll, and so ruined his opening gambit. "I just happened to be passing."

"Huh!" said Little My.

He looked first this way and then that in order to avoid her critical gaze. There was her raincoat hanging on a twig. And a cup with prunes and raisins in it. A bottle of fruit juice . . .

Moomintroll jumped up and leant forward. Further in under the branches the ground was flat with smooth pine-needles, and as far as his eyes could reach in the fog he saw rows and rows of tiny little crosses. They were made of broken sticks and bound together with twine. "What *have* you done?" he cried.

"Do you think this is where I bury all my enemies?" said Little My, much amused. "Those are birds' graves. Some-one's buried dozens of them in there."

"How do you know?" Moomintroll asked.

"I've looked," said Little My. "Small white skeletons, just like the one we found by the lighthouse the first day we were here. You remember, 'The Revenge of the Forgotten Bones'."

"It must have been the lighthouse-keeper," said Moomin-troll.

Little My nodded, and her tight little knot of hair shook.

"They must have flown into the light," Moomintroll said slowly. "It's what birds do . . . And killed themselves. Per-haps the lighthouse-keeper picked them up every morning. And then one day he got fed up with it, put the light out and went away. How frightful!" he cried.

"It's a long time ago," said Little My yawning. "The light's out now anyway."

Moomintroll looked at her and wrinkled his nose.

"You shouldn't feel so sorry for everything," she said. "Now run away. I'm going to take a nap."

When Moomintroll emerged from the thicket he opened his paw and looked at the horseshoe. He had said nothing about the little sea-horse. She was still his own.

*   *   *

There was no moon and the hurricane lamp wasn't lit, but all the same Moomintroll went down to the beach. He couldn't stop himself somehow. He had the horseshoe and the presents with him.

His eyes had grown accustomed to the darkness, and he saw the sea-horse as she came out of the fog like an unreal creature in a story. He put the horse-shoe down on the beach, hardly daring to breathe.

The shadowy form came nearer with small prancing steps. She stepped into her shoe in the absent-minded sort of way that ladies do, and stood there waiting for the shoe to fix itself firmly and start growing to her again with her head turned away from him.

"I like your fringe," said Moomintroll softly. "A friend of

mine has got one too. Perhaps she'll come and stay some day . . . I think you'd like lots of my friends."

The little sea-horse's silence showed she wasn't interested.

Moomintroll tried again. "Islands at night are so beautiful. This is Pappa's island, but I don't know if we shall live here all our lives. Sometimes I think that the island doesn't like us. The most important thing is that it should like Pappa . . ."

She wasn't listening. She didn't want to know about his family.

Then Moomintroll spread out his presents for her on the sand. The sea-horse came a little closer and sniffed them, but still she said nothing.

At last he found something to say. "You dance beautifully."

"Do you think so? Do you?" she said. "Have you been waiting for me? Have you really? You didn't expect me, did you?"

"Have I waited for you!" exclaimed Moomintroll. "I waited and waited and was so worried when it was so rough out there . . . I want to protect you from all danger! I have my own little nest and I have hung up your picture there. It's the only thing that I shall hang there . . ."

The sea-horse listened attentively.

"You're the most beautiful thing I've ever seen," Moomintroll went on, and just then the Groke began to howl.

There she was, sitting out there in the fog, howling for the lamp.

The little horse reared, and was gone, leaving behind her little pearls of laughter. A whole string of pearls followed her as she capered into the sea again.

The Groke came shuffling out of the fog towards where Moomintroll was standing. He turned and ran. But tonight the Groke didn't stop on the beach. She followed Moomintroll over the island, through the heather and right up to the lighthouse-rock. He could see her moving like a great grey shadow and then stop and crouch under the rock to wait.

Moomintroll slammed the door behind him and ran up the winding staircase with his heart in his stomach—it had happened: the Groke had come right on to the island!

Moominmamma and Moominpappa hadn't woken up and the room was quite quiet. But he could feel an uneasy feeling coming through the window as the island murmured in its sleep and turned over. He heard the poplar leaves rustle with fright and the gulls started to screech.

"Can't you sleep?" Moominmamma asked.

Moomintroll closed the window.

"I woke up," he said, and crept into bed. His nose was stiff with cold.

"It's getting colder," said Moominmamma. "It's a good thing I sawed up all those logs. Are you cold?"

"No," said Moomintroll.

She was sitting there freezing just below the lighthouse. She was so cold that the ground under her turned to ice . . . There it was again. It crept up and he couldn't shake it off. It was so easy to imagine somebody who could never get warm, somebody nobody liked, who destroyed everything wherever she went. It wasn't fair. Why should he have the Groke round his neck all the time, no one else had? You just *couldn't* help her to get warm!

"Are you unhappy about something?" Moominmamma asked.

"No," answered Moomintroll.

"Well, it'll be another nice long day tomorrow," said Moominmamma. "And it's all yours from beginning to end. Now isn't that a lovely thought!"

After a while Moomintroll knew that Moominmamma

had gone to sleep. He brushed all thoughts aside and started to play the game he played every night. At first he couldn't make up his mind whether to play the "Adventure" game or the "Rescue" game. Finally he decided on the "Rescue" game, it felt more real somehow. He shut his eyes and made his mind a blank. And then he started to think of a storm.

On a deserted rocky coast, rather like the island, the Storm was Raging. They were running up and down the beach, wringing their hands—someone was in Distress out there . . . Nobody dared to go out, it was quite impossible. Any boat would be Smashed to Pieces in an instant.

It wasn't Moominmamma that Moomintroll saved now, but the sea-horse.

Who was struggling out there? Was it the little Sea-horse with the Silver Shoe battling with a sea-serpent? No, that was too much. The Storm was quite enough.

The sky was all yellow, a real Storm-sky. And then he came along the beach himself. With great Determination he ran up to one of the boats . . . everybody started shouting: "Stop him! Stop him! He'll never do it! Lay hold of him!" He brushed them aside, got the boat out, rowed like mad. The Rocks stood out of the Sea like Great Black Teeth . . . but he felt no Fear. Little My was shouting something on the beach: "I didn't know he was so Brave! Oh, how sorry I am for everything. But it's Too Late! . . . Snufkin chewed his old pipe and murmured: "Farewell Old Pal." But he struggled on and on to where the little Sea-horse was just about to go down for the Third Time. He lifted her into the boat, and she lay there in a Heap, her wet Golden Hair round her. He took her safely to the beach, and it was remote and deserted. She whispered: "You have risked your Life to save mine. How Brave you are!" He smiled distantly and said: "I must leave you here. Our ways must part. My Destiny calls me,

Farewell!" The sea-horse stared at him in amazement as he
walked away. She was Impressed. "What?" she said.
"Would you leave me?" He waved to her as he walked on,
Alone, over the rocks in the Storm, getting smaller and
smaller . . . All those standing on the beach were astonished
and started to say to one another . . .

But at this point Moomintroll went to sleep. He sighed
happily and curled up like a ball under the warm, red
blanket.

*   *   *

"Where's the calendar gone to?" Moominpappa asked.
"I must make a cross on it, it's very important."

"Why?" said Little My as she climbed in the window.

"Well, we have to know what day it is," Moominpappa
explained. "We forgot to bring the clock with us, which was
a mistake. But things are impossible if one doesn't know
whether it's Sunday or Wednesday. No one can live like
that."

Little My drew in her breath through her nose and
breathed out through her teeth in that awful way of hers
which said "I've never heard anything so stupid in all my
life."

Moominpappa understood what she meant. So he was
already feeling good and angry when Moomintroll said:
"Actually, I borrowed it for a while."

"There are certain things which are extremely important
on an island like this," said Moominpappa. "Particularly
keeping the proper observations recorded in a log-book. One
must observe everything—nothing must be neglected. The
time, the direction of the wind, the level of the water, everything. You must hang up the calendar again immediately."

"All right! All right!" said Moomintroll loudly. He

swallowed his coffee and stamped down the stairs and out into the chilly autumn morning. The fog was still there. The lighthouse vanished into it like a huge pillar and the top of it was invisible. Up there, somewhere in the billowing fog, sat his family, just not understanding him. He was angry and sleepy, and just at the moment not the slightest bit interested in the Groke, the sea-horses, or his family either for that matter.

Just below the lighthouse-rock he woke up a bit. One might have thought it would happen—the Groke had chosen of all places to sit in Moominmamma's garden. He wondered whether she had sat there for longer than an hour. He hoped not. The rosebush was quite brown. For a moment Moomintroll's conscience hit him with its tail, but he was soon feeling angry and sleepy again. "Huh! Calendars indeed! Making crosses! What next!" How could an old troll like Moominpappa possibly understand that the picture of the sea-horse was a picture of Beauty itself that only he could see.

Moomintroll crept into the thicket and took the calendar

off its twig. The fog had made it all crinkled. He threw away the frame of flowers and sat down for a while, his head full of half-formed thoughts.

And suddenly he thought: "Why, I'll move here! They can live in that rotten old lighthouse with its awful stairs and count the days as they go by."

It was an exciting prospect, new, dangerous and wonderful. It changed everything. It seemed as though he was suddenly surrounded by a new melancholy, by strange possibilities.

He was stiff and cold when he got home. He put the calendar back on top of the desk. Moominpappa immediately went and made a cross in the top corner.

Moomintroll took a deep breath and said as boldly as he could: "I'm thinking of living somewhere else on the island by myself."

"Out of doors? Why, of course," said Moominmamma, not really paying much attention. She was sitting in the north window drawing a creeper. "That's all right. You can take your sleeping bag with you as usual." Now she was drawing honeysuckle, and it was very complicated. Moominmamma hoped she had remembered what it was really like. Honeysuckle doesn't grow by the sea. It needs a warm and sheltered spot.

"Mamma," said Moomintroll, and his throat felt very dry, "this isn't 'as usual'."

But Moominmamma wasn't listening. She made an encouraging sound and went on drawing.

Moominpappa was counting the crosses he had made. There was a Friday he wasn't quite sure about. He might have made two crosses that day because he had forgotten to make one on the Thursday. Something had disturbed him so that he wasn't quite sure about it. What had he done that day? The days floated together and went round and round in his head. It was like going round an island, walking for ever along the same beach without getting anywhere.

"All right!" said Moomintroll. "I'll take my sleeping-bag and the hurricane lamp."

Outside the window the fog swirled past. It seemed as though they were moving somewhere with the room.

"I really need a little blue," said Moominmamma to herself. She had made the honeysuckle grow out of the window and in again on the white wall, where it boldly opened out into a very carefully drawn flower.

The Waning Moon

One night just before dawn, Moominmamma was awakened by the silence round the lighthouse. It had suddenly become calm, as it can do when the wind is changing.

She lay for a long time listening.

Far out over the sea in the darkness a new wind started to blow very gently. Moominmamma could hear it approaching just like somebody walking over the water. It got stronger all the time, until it finally reached the island. The open window moved on its hooks.

Moominmamma felt very small as she lay there. She buried her nose in the pillow and tried to think of an apple tree. But she could only see the sea with its driving winds, a sea that swept the island when it lay all in the darkness, that was always everywhere, taking possession of the beach, the lighthouse and the whole island. She imagined that the whole world was smooth, gliding water and that very slowly the room itself was beginning to sail away.

"Imagine if the island came loose, and suddenly one morning was splashing in the water by the jetty back there at home. Or imagine if it glided further and further out and drifted for years and years until it fell over the edge of the world like a coffee cup on a slippery tray . . ."

"Little My would appreciate that," thought Moomin-mamma giggling to herself. "I wonder where she sleeps. And Moomintroll, too . . . What a pity mothers can't go off when they want to and sleep out of doors. Mothers, particularly, could do with it sometimes." She smiled to herself, and in an absent-minded way she sent Moomintroll a silent, loving greeting, in the way trolls do. Moomintroll, lying awake in his glade, felt that she had done this, and, as he usually did, wiggled his ears by way of answer.

No moon was shining, and it was very dark.

No one had made any fuss at all about his leaving home, and he wasn't quite sure whether he was relieved or disappointed.

Every evening after they had had tea, Moominmamma lit two candles and put them on the table and he took the hurricane lamp with him. Moominpappa said just for the sake of saying something: "Be careful not to set light to the thicket and make sure you put the lamp out before you go to sleep."

It was always the same. They hadn't understood one little bit.

Moomintroll lay listening to the wind, and thought: "The moon is on the wane. The sea-horse won't be here again for a long time."

But perhaps this was more of a relief than a disappointment. Now he could lie there just imagining lovely conversations with her and trying to remember what she looked like. And there was no need to be angry with the Groke any longer. She could stare at the lamp just as much as she wanted to. Moomintroll told himself that it was purely for practical reasons that he went to the beach every night with the lamp: to stop the Groke going right up to the lighthouse and ruining Moominmamma's roses. And so that the family shouldn't discover that she was there, too. To say nothing of stopping her howling. He didn't do it for any other reason.

Every night Moomintroll put the lamp on the beach and stood there yawning while the Groke gazed her fill.

She stared at the lamp, following a ritual of her own. After looking at it for a while she would begin to sing, or something that sounded like singing to her. It was a thin sound, something like humming and whistling together, and it penetrated everywhere, so that after a while Moomintroll felt that it was inside his head, behind his eyes, and even in his tummy. At the same time she swayed slowly and heavily from side to side, waving her skirts up and down until they looked like dry, wrinkled bats' wings. The Groke was dancing!

She was quite obviously very pleased, and somehow this absurd ritual became very important to Moomintroll. He could see no reason why it should stop at all, whether the island wanted it to or not.

But the island seemed to be getting more and more uneasy. The trees whispered and trembled, and great shudders went through the low-hanging branches, like the waves of the sea. The sea-grass on the beach shook and lay flat, trying to pull itself up by the roots in order to escape. One night Moomintroll saw something that made him feel afraid.

It was the sand. It had started to move. He could see it quite clearly, creeping slowly away from the Groke. There it was, a sparkling, glittering mass moving away from her great flat feet that were stamping the ground to ice as they danced.

Moomintroll grabbed the lamp and rushed as fast as he could into the thicket through the emergency tunnel. He got into his sleeping-bag, pulled the zip-fastener right up and tried to go to sleep. But however tightly he kept his eyes closed he could see nothing but sand creeping down the beach and into the water.

*   *   *

On the following day Moominmamma dug up four wild rose-bushes. They had twined their roots in among the stones in an almost terrifyingly patient way, and spread their leaves over the rock like an obedient carpet.

Moominmamma thought that pink roses against the grey of the rock would be perfectly lovely, but perhaps she hadn't given it enough thought when she planted them in her garden of brown seaweed. There they were, standing in a row looking most uncomfortable. She gave each of them a handful of the soil she had brought from home, watered them and then sat down beside them for a little while.

It was just then that Moominpappa came up to her, his
eyes wide with excitement, and shouted: "It's the black
pool! It's alive! Come and look, quickly!" Then he turned
and ran back towards it. Moominmamma got up and followed him, not understanding a word he had said. But
Moominpappa was right.

The dark water was rising and falling again—heaving
itself up and then sinking down again as if it was sighing
deeply. The black pool was breathing—it was alive.

Little My appeared, running over the rock. "Well," she
said, "Now something's going to happen. The island's coming to life! I always thought it would."

"Don't be so childish," said Moominpappa. "An island
can't come to life. It's the sea that's alive . . ." He became
silent and held his nose with both paws.

"Whatever is the matter?" Moominmamma asked
anxiously.

"I'm not sure," said Moominpappa. "I haven't really
thought it out yet. I had an idea just now, but I can't
remember what it was." He picked up the exercise-book and
wandered off over the rock, deep in thought.

Moominmamma stared at the black pool with a look of
extreme disapproval on her face.

"I think," she said, "that this is the right moment for us
all to go on a nice picnic."

And she went straight back to the lighthouse and started
to pack.

When she had got everything together that they would
need for a picnic, she opened the window and started to
bang the gong. She watched them all running towards the
lighthouse, not feeling the slightest bit guilty, although she
knew that the gong was only supposed to be used in cases of
extreme urgency.

She saw both Moominpappa and Moomintroll standing beneath her and looking up. From where she was they looked like two big pears. She held on to the window-sill and leaned out.

"Keep quite calm," she cried. "There's no fire! We're going on a picnic as soon as we possibly can."

"A picnic?" exclaimed Moominpappa. "How could you ring the bell just for a picnic?"

"There's danger in the air," Moominmamma shouted back. "If we don't go for a picnic this very instant, *anything* might happen to us!"

And they went for a picnic. With much effort the whole family hauled the *Adventure* out of the black pool. Then, rowing against the wind, they made for the largest of the outlying rocks on the north-west side of the island. Shivering, they pulled themselves up the wet rock and sat down. Moominmamma made a fire between some stones and began to get coffee ready. She did everything in exactly the same way as she had always done years and years ago. A table-cloth with four stones to hold it down, the butter-dish with its lid, their mugs, their bathing-towels looking like bright flowers spread out on the rock, and, of course, the sunshade too. Just as the coffee was ready it started to drizzle.

Moominmamma was in a very good mood. She talked all the time about ordinary everyday things, rummaged in the picnic basket and made sandwiches. It was the first time that she had got her handbag with her.

The rock they had come to was small and bare; there was nothing growing there at all, and no sign of seaweed or drift-wood. It was merely a bit of grey nothingness that just happened to be there in the water.

As they sat there drinking their coffee it seemed as if suddenly everything was perfectly natural and right. They began chatting about all sorts of things, but not about the sea, not about the island and not about Moominvalley.

From where they were, the island and the enormous light-house looked very strange, a remote grey shadow in the rain.

When they had finished their coffee, Moominmamma washed the mugs in the sea and put everything back in the basket. Moominpappa went to the water's-edge and started to sniff into the wind. "I think we ought to go back home now before the wind gets up," he said. It was what he always said when they went anywhere for a picnic. They bundled into the boat and Little My crept into the bows. On the way home the wind was behind them.

They pulled the *Adventure* up the beach.

Somehow the island was quite different once they were home again. They all felt it, but they said nothing. They didn't really know in what way it was different. Perhaps it was because they had left it for a while and then come back again. They went straight up to the lighthouse, and that evening they did the jigsaw puzzle, and Moominpappa made a little kitchen shelf and nailed it up beside the stove.

*   *   *

The picnic had done the family a lot of good, but some-how it had made Moominmamma a little sad. During the night she had dreamt that they had gone to see the Hatti-fatteners on an island off the coast near their old home, a green and friendly island, and when she had woken up in the morning she had felt sad.

When she was alone after breakfast, she sat quietly at the table looking at the honeysuckle growing over the window-sill. The indelible pencil had almost all gone, and what there was left of it Moominpappa needed for making crosses on the calendar and writing his notes.

Moominmamma got up and went up to the attic. When she came down again she had found three bags of dye, brown, blue and green, a tin of lead paint, a little lamp-black and two old paint-brushes.

So she began to paint flowers all over the wall. They were large, substantial flowers because the brushes were large, and the dye soaked right into the plaster and looked intense and transparent. How wonderful they looked! This was much more fun than sawing wood! Flower after flower appeared on the wall, roses, marigolds, pansies, peonies . . . No one was more surprised than Moominmamma herself. She had no idea she could paint so well. Near the floor she painted long, waving green grass, and she thought about putting the sun right at the top, but she had no yellow paint.

When the others came back for lunch she hadn't even lit the fire. She was standing on a box, painting a little brown bee with green eyes.

"Mamma!" exclaimed Moomintroll.

"What do you think of it?" Moominmamma asked, feeling very pleased with herself as she carefully finished the bee's second eye. But the brush was much too big, she would have to find some other way of doing it. If the worst came to the worst, she could paint over the bee and put a bird there instead.

"But it's all so life-like!" exclaimed Moominpappa. "I can recognise all those flowers! That one is a rose."

"No it isn't," said Moominmamma, very hurt. "It's a peony. Like the red ones we had at the bottom of the steps at home."

"Can I paint a hedgehog?" cried Little My.

Moominmamma shook her head. "No," she said. "This is my wall. But if you're good, I'll paint one for you."

At lunch everybody was very cheerful.

"You can lend me a little of that red-lead," Moomin-pappa said. "I must paint a low-watermark on the rock before the sea starts to rise again. I really must keep a serious check on the level of the water. You see, I want to find out whether the sea works to a system of some kind or whether it just behaves as it likes . . . It's very important."

"Have you made a lot of notes?" asked Moominmamma.

"Yes, lots. But I need a lot more before I can start writing my book." Moominpappa leant across the table and said confidentially: "I want to know if the sea is really obstinate, or whether it obeys."

"Obeys whom?" asked Moomintroll opening his eyes wide.

But Moominpappa was suddenly very busy eating his soup, and muttered: "Oh . . . something . . . rules of some kind or another."

Moominmamma gave him a little red-lead in a cup and he went out immediately after lunch to paint a low-water-mark.

*   *   *

The aspens had turned quite red, and in the glade the ground was covered with a yellow carpet of birch leaves. When the south-west wind blew it carried both red and yellow leaves out over the water.

On three sides of the hurricane lamp Moomintroll had painted the glass with lamp-black, just like some villain up to no good. He left the lighthouse by a roundabout way. It seemed to be following him with its vacant eyes. Evening was falling and the island was beginning to wake up. He could feel it stirring and hear the gulls crying round the point.

"I can't help it," he thought. "Pappa would understand if he knew. I don't want to see the sand moving tonight. Perhaps I'll go to the eastern end of the island this time."

Moomintroll sat on the rock and waited, with the hurricane lamp turned towards the sea. The island behind him was lost in the darkness, and there was no sign of the Groke.

Only Little My saw him. She saw the Groke too, sitting waiting on the beach.

Little My shrugged her shoulders and crept back under the moss. She had often seen people waiting for one another in the wrong place, looking foolish and lost. "Well, there's nothing to be done about it," she thought. "That's how it is."

The night was overcast. Moomintroll could hear invisible birds flying overhead and the sound of splashing behind him in the black pool. He turned, and in the ray of light from the lamp he could see them. It was the sea-horses, swimming below the cliff. Perhaps they had come here every night and he had known nothing about it.

The sea-horses were giggling and splashing each other with water and they made eyes at him from behind their fringes. Moomintroll looked from one to the other; they both had exactly the same eyes, the same flowers on their necks, and they both had the same saucy little heads. He had no idea which of them was his sea-horse.

"Is it you?" he asked.

The sea-horses swam towards him and stood at the edge of the water so that he could just see their knees.

"It's me! It's me!" they both replied and giggled like mad.

"Won't you rescue me?" one of them asked. "Won't you rescue me, my fat little sea-urchin. Do you gaze at my picture every single day? Do you?"

"He's not a sea-urchin," said the other one reproachfully. "He's a little egg-shaped mushroom who's promised to rescue me if it gets stormy. He's a little egg-shaped mushroom who collects shells for his mummy! It's charming, isn't it. Charming!"

Moomintroll felt himself blushing.

Moominmamma had polished the horseshoe with silver polish. He knew that one of the silver shoes was much brighter than the others.

And he knew, too, that they wouldn't lift their hooves out
of the water, and that he would never know which of them
was *his* sea-horse.

And they waded out to sea. He could hear them laughing,
and as they got farther and farther away the sound of their
laughter seemed to be nothing more than the wind sweeping
gently over the beach.

Moomintroll lay on the rock and stared at the sky. He

couldn't think of his sea-horse any more. Whenever he tried to he could see two sea-horses, two little sea-horses, both laughing and both exactly alike. All they did was leap up and down in the sea, until his eyes grew tired of looking at them. And there were more and more of them, so many he couldn't be bothered to count them. He just wanted to go to sleep and be left in peace.

*   *   *

Moominmamma's mural was more and more beautiful, and it stretched as far as the door. She had painted big green apple trees full of flowers and fruit, and the grass under the trees was full of windfalls. There were rose bushes all over the place, most of them red—just like the ones that grow in everybody's gardens. And each of them had a border of little white shells. The well was green and the woodshed was brown.

One evening when the sun was streaming into the room, Moominmamma was painting a corner of the veranda.

Moominpappa came into the room to have a look.

"Aren't you going to paint in some rocks?" he asked.

"There are no rocks," said Moominmamma absently. She was in the middle of painting the railings, and it was very difficult to get them straight.

"Is that the horizon?" continued Moominpappa.

Moominmamma looked up. "No. It's going to be the blue veranda," she said. "There's no sea here at all."

Moominpappa looked at it for a long time, but said nothing. Then he went and put the kettle on.

When he turned round again, he saw that Moominmamma had painted a large blue patch and above it something that was obviously meant to be a boat. It didn't look right at all.

"That's not so good," he said.

"It didn't turn out quite as I meant it to," admitted Moominmamma sadly.

"Well, it was a very nice idea," Moominpappa said consolingly. "But I suggest you try to change it into a veranda after all. It's no good trying to paint something you don't want to paint."

From that evening on Moominmamma's mural began to look more and more like Moominvalley. She found it difficult to get the perspective right sometimes, and sometimes she had to take something out of its proper setting and paint it all by itself. The stove and things out of the drawing-room, for example. And it was quite impossible to include every room. One could only paint one wall at a time, and somehow it looked unnatural.

Moominmamma found that the best time to paint was just before sunset. The room was empty then, and she could see Moominvalley much more clearly.

One evening the western sky was on fire with the most beautiful sunset she had ever seen. It was a tumult of red, orange, pink and yellow flames, filling the clouds above the dark and stormy sea with smouldering colours. The wind was blowing from the south-west towards the island from the sharp, coal-black line of the horizon.

Moominmamma was standing on the table painting apples on the top of a tree with red-lead paint. "If only I had these colours to paint with outside," she thought. "What lovely apples and roses I should have!"

As she gazed at the sky, the evening light crept up the wall, lighting up the flowers in her garden. They seemed to be alive and shining. The garden opened out, and the gravel path with its curious perspective suddenly seemed quite right and to lead straight to the veranda. Moominmamma put her paws round the trunk of the tree; it was warm with sunshine and she felt that the lilac was in bloom.

Like a flash of lightning a shadow passed across the wall. Something black had flown past the window. An enormous black bird was circling round and round the lighthouse, past one window after another, the west, the south, the east, the north . . . like a fury, beating its wings relentlessly.

"We're surrounded!" Moominmamma thought in confusion. "It's a magic circle. I'm scared. I want to go home and leave this terrible, deserted island and the cruel sea . . ." She flung her arms round her apple tree and shut her eyes. The bark felt rough and warm, and the sound of the sea disappeared. Moominmamma was right inside her garden.

The room was empty. The paints were still on the table, and outside the window the black bird went on circling round the lighthouse. When the colours in the western sky disappeared, it flew away across the sea.

When it was time for tea, the family came home.

"Where's Mamma?" Moomintroll asked.

"Perhaps she's just out getting some water," Moominpappa said. "Look, she's painted a new tree since we went out."

Moominmamma stood behind the apple tree and watched them making tea. They looked a little misty, as though she had been watching them moving about underneath the water. She wasn't at all surprised by what had happened. Here she was at last in her own garden where everything was in its proper place and everything was growing just as it should grow. Here and there something hadn't been drawn absolutely right, but it didn't matter. She sat down in the long grass and listened to the cuckoo calling from somewhere on the other side of the river.

When the kettle boiled for tea Moominmamma was fast asleep with her head leaning against the apple tree.

The South-West Wind

At dusk, the fisherman had a feeling that the beautiful big waves were coming. He dragged his boat high up the point and turned it over, and bound up his fishing-rods. Then he crept into his little house and curled himself up so that he looked like a wrinkled little ball. He lay there and allowed perfect solitude to surround him.

Of all winds the south-wester was his favourite. It had really settled in to blow and had not died down that evening at all. It was an autumn south-wester and could go on for weeks and weeks until the waves became high grey mountains heaving round the islands.

The fisherman sat in his house watching the sea swell. It was so marvellous not to have to care about a blessed thing. No one to talk and no one to ask questions, and no one to feel at all sorry for. Only the mystery and unfathomable vastness of the sea and the sky flooding over him and past him that could never disappoint him.

It was nearly dark when his perfect solitude was destroyed by Moomintroll coming over the slippery rocks. Moomintroll waved, made a loud noise and finally started to bang on

the window. He shouted as loud as he could that Moominmamma was lost. The fisherman smiled and shook his head.
The window-pane was much too thick to hear anything.

Moomintroll staggered on in the wind, waded back across
the point through the breakers and went towards the heather
to search there.

Moomintroll could hear his father calling, and he could
see the hurricane lamp swinging to and fro as Moominpappa
groped his way over the rock. The island was restless and
uneasy, full of strange whispers and cries, and as Moomintroll ran he was sure he could feel the ground moving
beneath his paws.

"Mamma's vanished," he thought. "She was so lonely,
she just disappeared."

Little My sat huddled up among the stones. "Look," she
said, "the stones are moving."

"I don't care," cried Moomintroll. "Mamma's lost!"

"Mammas don't get lost as easily as all that," said Little
My. "You can always find them in a corner somewhere if
you only look. I'm going to have a nap before the whole
island starts to slide away. Mark my words, there's going to
be a devilish to-do here before long!"

The hurricane lamp was over by the black pool, and
Moomintroll went over to it. Moominpappa turned round,
holding the lamp in the air.

"I do hope she hasn't fallen in . . ."

"It's all right, Mamma can swim," said Moomintroll.

They stood in silence for a moment, looking at each other.
The sea thundered on the lighthouse-rock.

"By the way," said Moominpappa. "Where have you
been living all this time?"

"Oh, just here and there," Moomintroll muttered, looking
in the other direction.

"I've had so much to see to," said Moominpappa vaguely.

Moomintroll could hear the stones turn themselves over. It was a strange, hard sound. "I'm going to look in the thicket," he said.

But just then two candles appeared in the window of the lighthouse. Moominmamma had come home.

When they came into the room she was sitting at the table making a towel.

"Where on earth have you been?" exclaimed Moominpappa.

"Me?" said Moominmamma innocently. "I was just taking a little stroll to get some air."

"But you mustn't frighten us like that," said Moominpappa. "You must remember that we're used to your being here when we come home in the evening."

"That's just it," Moominmamma sighed. "But one needs a change sometimes. We take everything too much for granted, including each other. Isn't that true, dearest?"

Moominpappa stared doubtfully at her, but she just laughed and went on sewing. So he went over to the calendar and made a cross on it to show that it was Friday. Below it he wrote: "Wind—force 5".

Moomintroll thought that the picture of the sea-horse had changed somehow. The real sea wasn't as blue as that, and the moon was a little overdone. He sat down at the table, and whispered as softly as he could: "Mamma. I'm living in a glade in the thicket."

"Are you?" said Moominmamma. "Is it nice there?"

"Yes, very. I thought perhaps that you might like to come and see it sometime."

"I'd love to," said Moominmamma. "When will you take me there?"

Moomintroll looked round quickly, but Moominpappa was deep in his exercise-book. Then he whispered: "Now. Straight away. Tonight."

"Ye—es," said Moominmamma. "But wouldn't it be nicer if we all went together in the morning?"

"It wouldn't be the same thing," said Moomintroll.

Moominmamma nodded her head and went on sewing.

Moominpappa wrote in his exercise-book: "Some things may change at night. For investigation: what does the sea do at night? Observations: my island is quite different in the dark because of (*a*) certain curious sounds, and (*b*) certain unmistakable movements."

Moominpappa lifted his pencil, hesitating for a moment. Then he continued: "Can strong emotional disturbance in a person transfer itself to his surroundings? Example: I was really very upset because we couldn't find Mamma. Investigate this."

He read through what he had written, and tried to come to some conclusion. But he couldn't, so he gave it up and pottered over to his bed.

Before he pulled the blanket over his head, he said: "Make

sure you turn the lamp out properly before you go to bed. We don't want it to smell."

"Of course, dearest," said Moominmamma.

*   *   *

When Moominpappa had gone to sleep, Moomintroll took the hurricane lamp and guided Moominmamma across the island. She stopped in the heather and listened.

"Is it always like this at night?" she asked.

"Yes, it does make you feel a little uneasy at night," Moomintroll said. "But you don't want to let that worry

you. It's only the island. You see, it wakes up at night just
when we're all asleep."

"I see," said Moominmamma. "Is that what it is."

Moomintroll led the way through the main entrance to
his glade. From time to time he looked round to make sure
that Moominmamma was still following. She got stuck in
the branches, but somehow she managed to reach the glade.

"So this is where you live!" she exclaimed. "How lovely
it is here!"

"The roof has lost most of its leaves," Moomintroll
explained. "But you should see it when it's green. It looks
just like a cave at the moment, with the lamp shining."

"Yes it does, doesn't it," said Moominmamma. "We
ought to bring a mat and a little box to sit on . . ." She
looked up and saw the stars and the clouds sailing past. "You
know," she said, "sometimes I get a feeling that this island
is moving, with us on it. We're drifting somewhere . . ."

"Mamma," said Moomintroll suddenly. "I've met the
sea-horses, but they don't seem to be interested in me at all.
I only wanted to run along the beach beside them, and
laugh with them, they're so beautiful . . ."

Moominmamma nodded her head. "I don't really think
it's possible to be friends with a sea-horse," she said gravely.
"It's not worth while being disappointed with them. I think
one is only meant to feel happy when one just looks at them
in the way that one looks at pretty birds or beautiful
scenery."

"Perhaps you're right," said Moomintroll.

They listened to the wind blowing through the thicket.
Moomintroll had quite forgotten the Groke.

"I'm sorry I've nothing to offer you," said Moomintroll.

"We've time for that tomorrow," said Moominmamma.
"We can have a little party in here, and the others can come

too if they want to. Well, it was nice to see where you live. Now I think I shall go back to the lighthouse."

*   *   *

After he had taken Moominmamma home, Moomintroll put out the hurricane lamp. He wanted to be alone. The wind was getting up. The darkness, the thundering of the sea, and something that Moominmamma had said, made him feel safe.

He came to the place where the rock fell away towards the black pool. He could hear the sound of the water splashing at the bottom of the cliff, but he didn't stop. He strolled on, feeling as light as a balloon and not the least bit sleepy.

And then he saw her. The Groke had come right up on to the island and she was nosing around below the lighthouse-rock. There she was, shuffling up and down, sniffing in the heather, and staring short-sightedly all round her. Then she wandered off towards the swamp.

"She's looking for me," thought Moomintroll. "But she might as well take it easy. I'm not going to light the lamp, it takes much too much paraffin."

He stood still for a moment, watching her wander forlornly over the island.

"She can dance tomorrow night," he said to himself with

a feeling of kindly indulgence. "But not just now. I feel like staying at home tonight."

So he turned his back on the Groke and took a roundabout route back to his glade.

*   *   *

Moomintroll woke at dawn with a feeling of panic. He was shut in. He was suffocating inside his sleeping-bag. Something was holding him down and he couldn't get his paws out. Everything felt upside down and he was surrounded by a curious brown light and a strange smell, as though he was deep down in the earth.

At last he managed to loosen the zip of his sleeping-bag. A cloud of soil and pine-needles was whirling round him, the whole world seemed changed, and he felt utterly lost. Everywhere, brown roots were creeping along the ground and right over his sleeping-bag. The trees weren't actually moving now, but in the darkness they had moved away from above his head. The whole forest had pulled up its roots and stepped over him just as though he was a stone. There was the match-box just where it always was and next to it the bottle of blackcurrant juice. But the glade had gone—it just wasn't there any more. The tunnels he had made had all grown over again. He seemed to be in a primeval forest, fleeing with the trees, creeping along the ground dragging his sleeping-bag. He had to hold on to it because it was a very fine sleeping-bag, and, besides, it had been given to him as a present.

He caught sight of the hurricane lamp. It was hanging in the tree where he had put it, but the tree had moved.

Moomintroll sat down and screamed for Little My at the top of his voice. She answered immediately. She gave a long series of signals in a voice that sounded like the clarion calls of a very small trumpet, or a buoy far out at sea. Moomin-troll started to crawl in the direction of the sound.

He came out into the daylight and the wind blew right in his face. He got up, his legs shaking, and looked at Little My with a feeling of intense relief. He thought that for once she was almost pretty.

A few of the smaller bushes which had pulled their roots out of the ground without any difficulty were already lying tangled and confused in the heather some way off. The swampy patch had sunk right into the ground and looked like a deep green ravine.

"What's happening?" Moomintroll cried. "Why are they pulling up their roots like that? I don't understand it."

"They're scared stiff," said Little My, looking at him right between the eyes. "They're so scared that every little pine-needle is standing on end. They're even more scared than you are! If I didn't know that in fact it's the other way round, I should think that the Groke had been here. Eh?"

Moomintroll felt a sinking feeling in his tummy and sat down in the heather. The heather was just the same as ever, thank goodness! It was flowering just as usual, and had decided to stay just where it was.

"The Groke," continued Little My thoughtfully. "Big, and cold, and wandering around, sitting down all over the place. And do you know what happens when she sits down?" Of course he knew. Nothing would grow. Nothing would ever grow where she had sat.

"Why are you staring at me like that?" Moomintroll exclaimed.

"Was I staring at you?" asked Little My innocently. "Why should I? Perhaps I was staring at something *behind* you . . ."

Moomintroll jumped up and looked round, terrified.

"Ha, ha! I was only pulling your leg!" cried Little My, delighted. "Isn't it funny how a whole island can go off its rocker and start moving? I think it's jolly interesting."

But Moomintroll didn't think it was funny. The thicket was moving towards the lighthouse, right across the island towards the lighthouse steps. It would get a little nearer every night until the first low-lying branch was pushing against the door and trying to get in.

"We won't open the door!" he said. Suddenly he looked at Little My right between the eyes. They were jolly eyes and they seemed to be laughing at him, as if to say: "I know all your secrets."

Somehow, this made him feel a lot better.

*   *   *

Immediately after breakfast, Moominpappa went out and sat on the lighthouse-keeper's ledge in the cliff. He was soon deep in all sorts of speculations.

The exercise-book was almost full of them. Speculations about the sea. The last heading he had added was: "The Way the Sea Changes at Night". He had underlined it. Now he sat there staring at the empty page below it as the wind tried to snatch it from between his paws. He sighed and turned the pages over until he came to page 5, of which he was particularly fond. On this page he had worked out that the black pool was connected to the sea by an unbelievably deep tunnel (shown on the map) and that it was through the tunnel that the treasure, the crates of whisky and the skeletons had unfortunately sunk to the bottom of the sea. The rusty canister had just happened to get stuck on the edge at the spot marked A. And if something or someone, for the sake of argument called X, had been at the point B and blown the water through the tunnel and then sucked it back

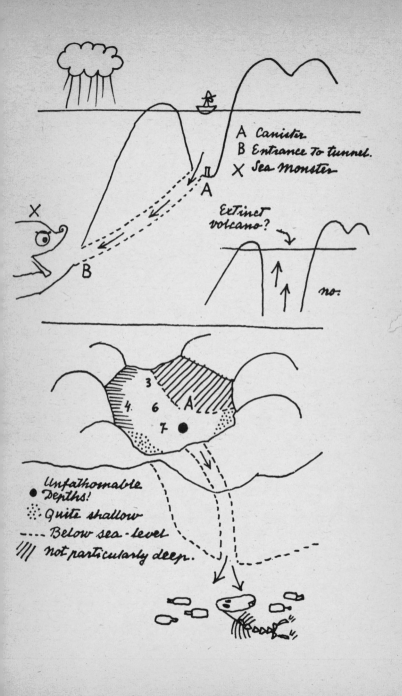

A Canister.
B Entrance to tunnel.
X Sea Monster

Extinct volcano?

no:

Unfathomable Depths!
Quite shallow
Below sea-level
Not particularly deep.

again, it would naturally rise and fall so that it seemed to be breathing. But who or what was X? A sea-monster? This couldn't be proved. He had transferred the whole question of the sea to the chapter entitled "Assumptions", now getting longer and longer.

In the chapter "Facts", Moominpappa maintained that water gets colder the deeper it is. He had known this before he had started, of course; he had only had to put his leg in the water to be aware of it. But with an ingeniously constructed bottle he had proved it conclusively. He also maintained that water was both heavy and salty. The deeper the water the heavier it was, and close to the surface it was much saltier. Proof: the shallow pools of salt water. They were very salty. And you could feel the weight of the water when you dived.

Seaweed is thrown up to leeward and not to windward. If you throw a plank into the wind from the lighthouse-rock, it doesn't come ashore but floats round the island a little way from the beach. If you hold a plank up against the horizon, the sky-line looks like the arc of a circle and not a straight line. In bad weather the water rises, but sometimes it does the opposite thing. Every seventh wave is enormous, but sometimes it is the ninth, and sometimes there doesn't appear to be any regular system.

And the long lines of foam that appear from nowhere just before a storm. Where did they come from, and where did they go to? Moominpappa tried to find an answer to these questions and lots of others, but it was very difficult. He began to feel very tired and unscientific, and wrote: "An island has no bridges and no fences, so it's impossible to be let out or to be shut in. This means that one feels . . ." No, it was no good. He crossed it out, and turned to the scanty chapter called "Facts".

The confusing thought that the sea obeyed no rules at all
returned. He tried to dismiss it from his mind quickly. He
was determined to understand, to solve the mystery of the
sea so that he would learn to like it and be able to keep his
self-respect.

*   *   *

While Moominpappa sat puzzling over these things,
Moominmamma was getting more and more absorbed with
her garden. She had discovered that a lot of things must be
painted again. Gradually she became bolder and bolder and
didn't hide behind one of the tree-trunks when she heard
the sound of footsteps on the stairs. Because she had noticed
that she became no bigger than a coffee-pot when she hid

herself among the trees on the wall, she painted lots of little Moominmammas all over the garden. Just in case one of the others caught sight of her—she had only to keep perfectly still and they couldn't tell which was the real Moomin-mamma.

"Well, that really is the last word in madness," said Little My. "Couldn't you paint some of us and not just yourself?"

"But you're outside on the island," said Moominmamma.

She had asked Moomintroll about having a party in his glade, but he had only muttered something and gone out.

"It's the sea-horse," Moominmamma said to herself. "Ah! well, that's how it is!" and she painted yet another Moomin-mamma, this time sitting under the lilac bush and enjoying herself.

Moomintroll went slowly down the stairs and out on to the lighthouse-rock. The glade had disappeared and there were no sea-horses any longer.

He stood looking at Moominmamma's garden at the bottom of the rock. The rose-bushes had all withered because they had been moved to such a soft spot and no longer had the sand and the stones to lean on. Moominmamma had put up a little fence in the middle of the flower-bed which was supposed to enclose something. Quite what it was, Moomin-troll couldn't think. Something she was trying to grow there.

Little My came rushing up to him. "Hallo," she said. "Do you know what? Give you three guesses."

"No, tell me," said Moomintroll.

"It's an apple," announced Little My. "She's planted an apple that floated ashore. She says that the seeds will grow into an apple tree."

"An apple!" repeated Moomintroll in surprise. "But it takes years and years for an apple tree to grow!"

"You bet it does!" said Little My, and rushed off.

Moomintroll remained where he was and studied the fence. It had been very well made and looked remotely like the railings of the veranda at home. He began to chuckle to himself. It was a nice feeling, it felt good to laugh. No one was quite as stubborn as Moominmamma. He wondered whether she would get her apple tree after all. She deserved to. And from one thing to another, it would actually be much more fun to have a tiny little cottage than a glade. A tiny little cottage one had built with one's own paws. One could put pretty little pebbles in the window.

*   *   *

Moominpappa and Moominmamma didn't notice that the forest was moving decidedly closer to the lighthouse until some time during the afternoon. The alders seemed to have been in more of a hurry than the other trees, and they had crept halfway up the island. Only the alder to which the *Adventure* was tied remained, although it had nearly strangled itself by straining at the rope. The aspens had lost all their leaves and could no longer rustle with fright. Instead they had flung themselves into the heather in terrified little groups.

The trees all looked like insects, trying to tie their roots in knots round the stones and gripping the heather in a desperate attempt to hold on against the south-west wind.

"But what does it mean?" whispered Moominmamma looking at Moominpappa. "Why do they do it?"

Moominpappa bit his pipe and desperately tried to find some sort of explanation. It was awful to be forced to say: "I don't know". He was fed up with not understanding anything.

Finally he said: "It's the sort of thing that happens at

night. Things can change during the night, you know."

Moominmamma stared at him.

"It's just possible that," continued Moominpappa nervously, "that . . . er . . . some sort of secret transformation in the darkness, I mean . . . if we were to go outside and . . . er . . . add to the confusion, it would be so great . . . the confusion I mean . . . er . . . that when we woke up in the morning everything would be just as it was . . ."

"What *are* you talking about, dearest?" asked Moominmamma anxiously.

Moominpappa blushed scarlet.

After an embarrassed pause, Moomintroll murmured: "They're scared."

"Do you think so?" said Moominpappa gratefully. "Yes, I think you've got something there . . ." He looked round at the scarred ground. Every single tree had moved away from the sea.

"At last I understand!" exclaimed Moominpappa. "They're scared of the sea. The sea frightened them. I *felt* something going on when I was out last night . . ." He opened his exercise-book and fumbled with the pages. "This is what I wrote down this morning . . . just a minute. I must think about this very carefully . . ."

"Will it take long?" Moominmamma asked.

But Moominpappa was already on his way to the light-house-rock with his nose deep in his notes. He tripped over a bush, and then disappeared among the trees.

"Mamma," said Moomintroll. "I don't think this is anything to worry about. The trees just go a little way and then take root again and grow in the usual way."

"Do you think so?" said Moominmamma in a hushed voice.

"Perhaps they'll make a little arbour round your garden,"

said Moomintroll. "It would look nice, wouldn't it? Lots of little birch trees with pale-green leaves . . ."

Moominmamma shook her head and started to walk towards the lighthouse. "It's nice of you to say so," she said. "But I just don't think it's a natural way of behaving. The trees at home never did anything like that."

She decided to go and sit in her garden for a while and calm down.

Moomintroll released the alder from the rope of the *Adventure*. The south-west wind was much stronger now and the sky was bright and clear and the breakers over by the western end of the island were higher and whiter than he had ever seen them. Moomintroll went and lay in the heather. He felt quite peaceful, almost cheerful. What a relief it was that Moominpappa and Moominmamma had at last noticed what had happened!

A solitary bee buzzed gently from blossom to blossom in the heather. The heather didn't seem to be afraid of anything. It just went on growing in the same place. "What if I should build my tiny little cottage just here!" thought Moomintroll. "Very close to the ground, and with flat stones in front of the door."

He woke up as something cast its shadow over him. Moominpappa was standing beside him looking very worried.

"Well?" asked Moomintroll.

"It's no good," answered Moominpappa. "This business of the trees spoils everything. I understand the sea less than ever. There's no system or order in things at all." He took off the lighthouse-keeper's hat and began to crumple it up, twist it and then smooth it out again.

"You see," said Moominpappa, "my idea is to discover what secret rules the sea obeys. I must if I'm going to learn

to like it. I shall never be happy on this island until I've
learned to like the sea."

"It's exactly the same with people," said Moomintroll
eagerly, sitting up. "Liking them, I mean."

"The sea is all the time changing the way it behaves,"
continued Moominpappa. "It seems to do just what it likes.
Last night it terrified the whole island. Why? What happened? There's just no rhyme or reason in it. And if there *is*,
it's more than I can understand."

He looked inquiringly at Moomintroll.

"I'm sure you'd understand if there was," said Moomintroll. He was very flattered to think that Moominpappa
should discuss such terribly important things with him, and
made a tremendous effort to understand what it was all
about.

"Do you really think so?" Moominpappa said. "You mean
you don't think there's any rhyme or reason in it all?"

"I'm sure there isn't," replied his son, desperately hoping
he had said the right thing.

Some gulls rose from the point, and began to circle over
the island. They could feel the breakers underneath them,
like someone breathing in the ground.

"But the sea must be a living thing, then," mused
Moominpappa. "It can think. It behaves exactly as it feels
inclined . . . it's impossible to understand it. . . If the forest is
afraid of the sea it must mean that the sea is alive, surely?"

Moomintroll nodded. His throat felt quite parched he
was so excited.

Moominpappa was silent for a moment. Then he got up
and said: "Then it's the sea that's breathing in the black
pool. It's the sea that tugs at the plumb-line. Everything's
quite clear. It went off with my breakwater, it filled my nets
with seaweed and tried to upset the boat . . ."

He stood staring at the ground, his nose all wrinkled with a frown. Then suddenly his face cleared and he said with a feeling of great relief: "Then I don't *need* to understand! The sea's just a weak character you can't rely on . . ."

Moomintroll thought that Moominpappa was just talking to himself, so he said nothing. He watched him walk towards the lighthouse, leaving his exercise-book behind him in the heather.

There were lots more birds in the sky now, and they

screamed as if possessed. Moomintroll had never seen so
many birds all at once. The sky was almost black with them,
little ones too, and they whirled round overhead wildly,
more and more of them coming in from over the sea.
Moomintroll gazed at them. He knew that they, too, were
fleeing from the Groke and her dreadful coldness. But there
was nothing he could do about it. But what did it matter,
anyway? Pappa had talked to him in quite a new way, and
he felt tremendously proud.

The others were standing outside the lighthouse staring at
the birds that seemed to fill the sky with their terrified cries.
Then in a flash they flew off over the sea. The birds had gone,
right out to sea, leaving nothing behind but the sound of the
breakers.

The sea thundered in over the island, flinging the spray
so high that it seemed to be snowing. Over at the western end
of the island the waves looked like white dragons with gaping
jaws.

"I bet the fisherman's pleased," Moomintroll thought.

Just at that moment it happened. He saw the fisherman's
little house of cement topple over, and the next wave washed
away the walls.

The fisherman had managed to open the door in time, and
dashed out like greased lightning through the foam. He crept
under his boat, which was lying upside down on the rock.
Nothing remained of the little house now except the iron
clamps, sticking out of the rock like left-over teeth.

"Well, bless my tail!" Moomintroll thought. "Pappa was
right. The sea is *really* bad-tempered!"

                    ★   ★   ★

"But he must be soaked to the skin!" exclaimed
Moominmamma. "And he may well be full of splinters of

glass from the window . . . WE must look after him, now that
he's got nowhere to live!"

"I'll go and see how he is," said Moominpappa. "I fully
intend to defend my island!"

"But the whole point is under water, it's dangerous!"
Moominmamma cried. "You might get washed away by the
waves . . ."

Moominpappa leapt up and grabbed his plumb-line,
which was hanging up under the stairs. He was exhilarated.
He felt as light as air.

"Don't be afraid," he said. "The sea can do what it likes.
Let it do its worst, I don't care! I intend to protect every
single person living on this island!"

Moominpappa went down the rock with Little My dancing round him. She shouted something, but it was lost in the

wind. Moomintroll stood in the heather gazing at the spot where the fisherman's house had been.

"You can come, too," said Moominpappa. "It's high time you learnt to defend yourself!"

They ran across the island to the point, now under water. Little My was jumping up and down with excitement. Her hair, loosened by the wind, was blowing round her head like a halo.

Moominpappa looked at the angry sea, breaking over the island, throwing up spray and falling back again with a terrible sucking sound. And over the point the waves were thundering. It was here that they would have to cross. Moominpappa tied the rope round his waist and passed the end to his son.

"Now hold on to this like grim death," he said. "Make a good knot and follow after me with the rope taut. We'll fool the sea! The wind's force seven! Force seven!"

Moominpappa waited until a huge wave had broken and then made for a rock sticking out of the water a little way away. It was dangerously slippery wherever he put his paws, but when the next wave broke he had passed the rock. The rope between him and Moomintroll tightened, the sea swirled under their paws, and turned them head over heels in the water. But the rope held.

When the wave had passed, they slid across the boulders and repeated the manœuvre at the next big rock.

"It's high time you learnt some manners!" thought Moominpappa, meaning the sea, of course. "There's a limit to everything . . . it doesn't matter how much of a nuisance you make of yourself to us, we can put up with it. But to pick on that fisherman, poor wrinkled piece of seaweed that he is, when he admires you so much, is going a bit too far. It's really quite upsetting . . ."

A mountainous wave broke over him, washing away his anger.

He was nearly across. The rope tightened round his waist. He grabbed the side of a rock and held on tight with all four paws. Yet another wave washed over him, and the rope went slack.

As soon as he got his nose out of the water, Moominpappa clambered up the point as quickly as he could. His paws were shaking. He began to haul the rope in with his son on the end. Moomintroll was bobbing up and down a little way off to leeward.

They sat next to each other on the rock shivering with cold. On the other side Little My was bouncing up and down like a ball, obviously cheering them like mad. Moomintroll looked at Moominpappa and they started to laugh. They had fooled the sea.

"How goes it?" shouted Moominpappa, sticking his nose under the fisherman's boat. The fisherman turned his bright blue eyes towards him. He was drenched to the skin, but had escaped the flying glass from the window.

"Do you feel like a nice cup of coffee?" Moominpappa shouted above the noise of the wind.

"I don't know, it's such a long time since I had one . . ." The fisherman's voice sounded like a cracked tin whistle. Suddenly Moominpappa felt terribly sorry for him. He was so small, he couldn't possibly manage to get home by himself.

Moominpappa stood up and looked at Moomintroll. He shrugged his shoulders and pulled a face, as if to say: "Well, that's how it is; there's nothing much we can do about it." Moomintroll nodded his head.

They began to walk as far as they could towards the point. The wind flattened their ears against the sides of their heads, and the salt spray made their faces smart. When they could walk no further Moominpappa and Moomintroll stopped and looked at the stately column of foam that rose in front of them with every wave, rising slowly, almost ceremoniously, and then falling back into the sea.

"It's an enemy worth fighting, anyway," shouted Moominpappa through the noise of the breakers.

Moomintroll nodded his head. He hadn't heard what Moominpappa had said, but he understood all the same.

Something was being carried to the shore by the waves. It was a box. It was floating to leeward on one side of the point and was lying heavy in the water. It was strange how they understood each other without exchanging a word. Moomintroll jumped in and let himself be carried towards the box by a retreating wave while Moominpappa braced himself against the rock.

Moomintroll reached the box. It was heavy and had a handle made of rope. He could feel the line round his waist tighten as he was hauled to the shore again. It seemed to him that he was playing the most exciting and dangerous game he had ever played, and, what's more, he was playing it with his own pappa.

They dragged the box ashore. It was intact. They discovered that it was a crate of whisky from some foreign land. They could tell from the outlandish designs on the outside in red and blue.

Moominpappa turned his eyes towards the sea, half in surprise and half in admiration. The waves were a deeper green now and the evening sun shone on their crests.

*   *   *

After the fisherman had fortified himself with a good strong whisky, they helped him across to the island. Moominmamma was standing there waiting for them with the lighthouse-keeper's old clothes over her arm. She had found them in the bottom drawer of the desk.

"I don't like those trousers,"

said the fisherman, his teeth chattering.

"I think they're ugly."

"You just go behind one of these boulders and put them on," said Moominmamma firmly. "It makes no difference whether you think they're ugly or not. They're warm and, what's more, they once belonged to a perfectly respectable lighthouse-keeper, and there's nothing wrong with them, or with him for that matter, although he seems to have been a very melancholy sort of man."

She put the clothes over the fisherman's arm and made him go behind a boulder.

"We've found a crate of whisky," Moomintroll told her.

"Splendid!" said Moominmamma. "Then we must go for a picnic!"

Moominpappa laughed. "You and your picnics," he said.

After a while the fisherman reappeared in a corduroy jacket and a pair of battered old trousers.

"But they look as if they were made for you," exclaimed Moominmamma. "Now I think we should all go home and have a nice cup of coffee."

Moominpappa noticed that she had said "home" and not "the lighthouse". It was the first time she had done it.

"Oh, no!" cried the fisherman. "Not there!" He looked at his trousers in terror, and made off over the island as fast as his legs could carry him. They watched him disappear into the thicket.

"You'll have to take him some coffee in a thermos," said Moominmamma to Moomintroll. "Have you pulled that crate up so that it will be safe?"

"Don't worry," said Moominpappa. "It was a present from the sea, and not even the sea would take a present back."

*   *   *

They drank tea a little earlier that evening.

Afterwards they took out the jigsaw puzzle and Moominmamma fetched the tin of toffees from the mantelpiece.

"It's a very special day today, so you can have five each," she said. "I wonder whether the fisherman likes toffees."

"You know what," said Moominpappa. "I never felt really happy about the toffees you put out for me on the rock."

"Why not?" asked Moominmamma, surprised. "You are very fond of toffees, aren't you?"

"Nonsense!" said Moominpappa with an embarrassed laugh. "It may have been because I couldn't get anywhere with my investigations. I don't know."

"You just felt a stupid fool, that's all," put in Little My. "Can I count two toffees as one if they're stuck together? Are you going to stop bothering about the sea, then?"

"Far from it," exclaimed Moominpappa. "Do I stop bothering about you just because you behave like a stupid fool?"

They all laughed.

"You see," Moominpappa said, leaning forward, "the sea is sometimes in a good temper and sometimes in a bad temper, and nobody can possibly understand why. We can only see the surface of the water. But if we *like* the sea, it doesn't matter. One learns to take the rough with the smooth . . ."

"Oh, you *like* the sea now, do you?" asked Moomintroll shyly.

"I've always liked the sea," said Moominpappa indignantly. "All of us like it. That's why we came here, isn't it?" He looked at Moominmamma.

"Yes, I suppose so," she said. "Look, I've found a bit that fits into that awkward spot."

They all bent over the puzzle admiringly.

"It's going to be a big grey bird!" exclaimed Little My. "There's the tail of another—a white one. They're flapping their wings as though someone had lit a match under them!"

Now that they had discovered what the puzzle was supposed to be, they soon found four birds. It began to get dark and Moominmamma lit the hurricane lamp.

"Are you going to sleep outside tonight?" she asked.

"Not on your life," answered Little My. "Our hide-outs have all grown over."

"I'm thinking of building a tiny little house of my own," Moomintroll announced. "Not immediately, but sometime anyway. When it's ready you can all come and call."

Moominmamma nodded her head. She was adjusting the flame of the lamp. "What's the wind like now? Have a look and see, dear, will you?" she said to Moominpappa.

He went over to the north-window and opened it. After a while he said: "I can't see whether the forest's moving or not. It's blowing just as hard. It's probably up to force eight."

He shut the window and came back to the table.

"The trees will be on the move later tonight," said Little My, her eyes sparkling. "Moaning and groaning and groping higher and higher up the rock—like this!"

"You don't think they'll try and get in here, do you?" Moomintroll exclaimed.

"Of course they will," said Little My, lowering her voice. "Can't you hear the boulders beating against the door downstairs? They're rolling up from all directions, crowding round the door. The trees are closing in round the lighthouse, getting nearer and nearer. Then their roots will start climbing up the walls until they're right outside these windows making it dark inside . . ."

"No, stop!" cried Moomintroll, putting his paws round his nose.

"Really, my dear," said Moominmamma. "Please don't imagine such things!"

"Please keep calm, all of you!" said Moominpappa. "There's no cause for alarm. Just because a few poor little bushes are scared of the sea there's no need to get worked up about it. It's really much worse for the bushes, you know. I shall see to the matter."

It began to get darker and darker, but no one thought of going to bed. They found three more birds, and Moominpappa was absorbed in a drawing of a kitchen cupboard.

The storm raging outside made the room feel very safe. From time to time one of them said something about the fisherman, wondering whether he had found the thermos and drunk the coffee.

Moomintroll began to feel uneasy. It was time for him to go and see the Groke. He had promised her she could dance tonight. He huddled up in his chair and said nothing.

Little My looked at him, her eyes like shiny black beads. Suddenly she said: "You left the rope down on the beach."

"The rope?" Moomintroll said. "But I brought . . ."

Little My kicked him viciously under the table. He got up and said very sheepishly: "Why, so I did. I must go and fetch it. If the water rises it'll get washed away."

"Go carefully," said Moominmamma. "There are so many roots everywhere, and we've only got one glass for the lamp. And while you're out you can have a look for Pappa's exercise-book."

Moomintroll looked at Little My before he closed the door behind him. But she was busy with the jigsaw puzzle, whistling nonchalantly between her teeth.

The Lighthouse-Keeper

The island was moving all night. The fisherman's point drifted imperceptibly a little farther out to sea.

Shudder after shudder shook the whole island like chills running up and down its spine, and the black pool seemed to creep deeper and deeper into the rocks. It was sucked in and out and fresh waves broke in from the sea, but the pool never seemed to fill up. Its enormous mirror-like black eye sank lower and lower, surrounded by a fringe of sea-grass round the edges.

On the beach on the leeward side, little field-mice ran backwards and forwards at the edge of the water, the sand slipping away from under their paws. Boulders turned over heavily, revealing the pale roots of the sea pinks.

At dawn the island slept. The trees had reached the light-house-rock, deep holes were left where great boulders had been before, now lying scattered among the heather. They were waiting for another night to come so that they could roll nearer and nearer the lighthouse. The great autumn gale continued to blow.

At seven o'clock Moominpappa went out to look at the boat. The water had risen again and the south-west wind was blowing the sea higher and higher. He found the fisherman lying rolled up at the bottom of the *Adventure*. He was playing with a handful of pebbles. He blinked under his fringe, but he said nothing. And the *Adventure* lay there beaten by the waves and without a mooring.

"Can't you see that this boat is about to drift out to sea?" said Moominpappa. "She's being bashed against a stone. Just look at it! Come on now! Jump out and give me a hand to pull her up!"

The fisherman twisted his bent legs over the side of the boat and tumbled on to the beach. His eyes were just as kind and gentle as ever, and he said: "I haven't done any harm . . ."

"You haven't done any good, either," said Moominpappa; with a tremendous effort he pulled the boat up himself.

He sat down on the sand, puffing and blowing. What was left of the sand, that is. The angry sea seemed to be jealous of the sand, taking more and more of it away every night. He looked at the fisherman sourly and said: "Did you find the coffee?"

But the fisherman only smiled.

"There's something wrong with you that I can't make out," Moominpappa said to himself. "You're not a human being at all. You're more like a plant or a shadow, just as if you'd never been born."

"I was born," the fisherman said immediately. "It's my birthday tomorrow." Moominpappa was so surprised that he began to laugh.

"You remember that all right," he said. "So you have a birthday, do you? Just think! And how old are you, if I may ask?"

But the fisherman turned his back and strolled off along the beach.

Moominpappa went back to the lighthouse. He felt very worried about his island. The ground where the forest had been was abandoned and full of deep holes. Long furrows crossed the heather, left by the trees as they moved towards the lighthouse-rock. And there they stood, a tangled skein of fright.

"I wonder what one has to do to calm an island down," Moominpappa wondered. "It won't do for the island and the sea to fall out with each other. They must be friends . . ."

Moominpappa stood still. There was something wrong with the lighthouse-rock. With a very slight movement it was shrinking, like skin going into wrinkles. A couple of grey boulders turned over in the heather. The island seemed to be waking up.

Moominpappa listened. A chill went down his spine. He was sure he could feel it. A very slight thumping sound. He could feel it all over his body, getting closer. It seemed to come from deep down in the ground.

Moominpappa lay down in the heather and pressed his ear to the ground. He could hear the island's heart beating. It was deeper than the sound of the breakers, deep deep down in the earth, a soft dull heart-beat.

"The island is alive," Moominpappa thought. "My island is just as much alive as the trees and the sea. Everything is alive."

He got up slowly.

A juniper was creeping quietly through the heather like an undulating green carpet. Moominpappa scrambled out of its way, and stood stock-still, frozen to the spot. He could see the island moving, a living thing crouching on the bottom of the sea, helpless with fear. "Fear is a terrible thing," Moominpappa thought. "It can come suddenly and take hold of everything, and who will protect all the little creatures who come in its way?" Moominpappa started to run.

He got home, and hung his hat on its nail.

"What's the matter?" asked Moominmamma. "Has the boat . . .?"

"I pulled her up," said Moominpappa. The family stared at him and he added: "It's the fisherman's birthday tomorrow."

"No? Really?" Moominmamma exclaimed. "Is that why you're looking so strange? Well, we must give a party for him. Imagine! Even the fisherman has a birthday!"

"It'll be easy to think of a present for him," said Little My. "Little parcels full of sea-grass, a lump of moss, or just a damp spot, perhaps!"

"Now you're not being very nice," Moominmamma said.

"But I'm not nice," cried Little My.

Moominpappa stood at the window, looking out over the island. He could hear his family discussing two very important questions: how to get the fisherman to come into the lighthouse and how to get the crate of whisky over the sea-washed point. But he could only think of the island's timid heart-beats deep down in the ground.

He would have to talk to the sea about it.

*   *   *

Moominpappa went and sat on the lighthouse-keeper's

ledge in the cliff, looking as though he was the figure-head in the bows of his galleon—the island.

This was the real storm he had waited for, but it wasn't what he had imagined it would be. No beautiful pearls of foam on the waves, no, not in a wind force eight. Instead the foam was blown off the surface of the sea like angry grey smoke, and the water was lined and furrowed like a face wrinkled with rage.

Suddenly, in the way it can happen to a troll, Moominpappa found it terribly easy to start talking to the sea— silently, of course.

"You're much too grown-up to show off like this, it's unworthy of you. Is it really so important to you to frighten a poor little island like this? It has a tough enough time right out here as it is. You ought to be happy that it's here. What fun would you have without its rocks to wash your breakers over? Think carefully, now! Here's a little tuft of trees, growing all bent for your sake. And a handful of scanty soil which you do your best to wash away, and a few rugged rocks which you polish so smooth that there's hardly anything left of them. And then you've the nerve to frighten them!"

Moominpappa leant forward and stared sternly at the fuming sea. "There's something you don't seem to understand," he said. "It's your job to look after this island. You should protect and comfort it instead of behaving as you do. Do you understand?" Moominpappa listened, but the sea made no answer.

"You've tried it on with us, too," he said. "You've pestered us in every way you can, but it hasn't worked. We're getting along somehow, in spite of you. I've learnt to understand you, and that's what you don't like, do you? And we haven't given up, have we? By the way," Moomin-

pappa continued, "to be perfectly fair, it was jolly decent of you to give us that crate of whisky. I know why you did, you know when you're beaten, don't you? But to get your own back by taking it out of the island was a petty thing to do. Now, I'm only saying all this because—well—because I like you."

Moominpappa was silent. He felt tired, and leant back

against the cliff and waited. The sea said nothing. But a large shiny plank of wood was drifting towards the shore, bobbing up and down on the waves.

Moominpappa regarded it excitedly.

There was another one, and another and another. Someone had thrown a whole boat-load of them overboard.

He climbed up the cliff and started to run, laughing to himself. The sea was saying it was sorry. It wanted them to stay. It wanted to help them to go on building on the island. It wanted them to settle down there and enjoy themselves although they were surrounded by a vast, never-changing horizon closing in on them.

"Come outside, all of you!" he shouted up the winding staircase. "Driftwood! Lots of it! Come and help me to salvage it!"

The whole family came tumbling out.

The planks drifted towards the leeward side of the island, carried along by the heaving swell. In no time at all they would drift on past the island. They would have to be quick. They threw themselves into the sea, unconscious of the cold water. Perhaps they had some pirate blood in their veins that made them plunge in like that, the spirit of some ancestor out for ill-gotten gains seemed to possess them. They seemed to be throwing off the melancholy of the island and the loneliness of the sea as they went in and out of the water, carrying and stacking the planks and shouting to each other over the roar of the waves. The sky above them was still sparkling and cloudless.

It's an exciting job trying to manœuvre a two-inch plank ashore. It's unmanageable and heavy with water, and can so easily get away and then hit you with the force of a battering-ram when it is carried in by the next wave. Then it is really dangerous.

And when it is lying on the beach out of the sea's reach it becomes treasure-trove. Shining and with the warm colour of old tar, it lies at your feet, and you can read the owner's mark at one end. With the proud satisfaction of the conqueror you begin to think of three-inch nails and the sound of them being hammered in.

"The wind must be at least force nine now!" cried Moominpappa. He took a deep breath and looked at the sea. "Good!" he said. "Now we're even!"

When all the planks were piled up on the beach, the family went home to make some fish-soup. Like a living force the storm continued to rage, and Little My could only just keep on her feet.

Moominmamma stopped when she came to her garden, now hidden under a mass of branches. She got down on her knees and looked underneath them.

"Is the apple tree coming up?" Moomintroll asked.

"I'm not quite as stupid as all that!" said Moominmamma

with a laugh. "I just thought it needed a little encouragement, that's all."

She looked at her withered rose-bushes and thought: "How silly of me to put them there! But there are plenty, the island is full of them, and anyway, wild flowers are even more beautiful than garden flowers, perhaps."

*   *   *

Moominpappa had dragged a few planks up the stairs and got out his tool-box. "I know wood shrinks when it dries," he said. "But I can't wait. You don't mind if there are a few cracks in the kitchen shelves, do you?"

"Not at all," said Moominmamma. "Go ahead. Hammer away while you feel like it!"

She had painted nothing that day. Instead she had made a few little sticks to support the flowers and tidied up the desk. She had even tidied up the lighthouse-keeper's drawer. Moomintroll was sitting at the table drawing. He knew exactly what his little house should look like. There wasn't a great deal left of the indelible pencil, but somehow he felt sure that the sea would wash one ashore when needed.

Towards evening they all felt a little tired and didn't say much to each other. Inside, it was very peaceful. They could hear the sea thundering rhythmically round the island, and the sky was as white as if it had been newly washed. Little My had fallen asleep on the stove.

Moominmamma gave them a quick look and walked over to her mural. She pressed her paws against the trunk of the apple tree. Nothing happened. It was only a wall, just an ordinary plaster wall.

"I just wanted to know," thought Moominmamma. "I was right. Of course I can't get into this garden any more. I'm not homesick now."

*　　　　*　　　　*

At dusk Moomintroll went to fill the hurricane lamp.

The can of paraffin was underneath the stairs with a pile of torn nets. He put a tin under the hole in the top and took out the stopper. When he lifted the can it rattled, making a strange echoing sound. He held it over the tin and waited. He shook the can.

Then he put it down and stood staring at the floor for a moment. There was no more paraffin. It was finished. The lamp had been burning every night in the room upstairs and every night it had shone for the Groke. Apart from that Little My had poured several pints over the ants. What was he to do? What would the Groke say? He daren't think how disappointed she would be. He sat on the stairs with his nose in his paws.

He felt as though he had let her down.

*　　　　*　　　　*

"Are you absolutely certain the whole can's empty?" Moominmamma asked, giving the lamp a good shake.

They had finished their tea, and the windows were getting dark.

"Quite empty," said Moomintroll wretchedly.

"It must be leaking," said Moominpappa. "Perhaps it's getting rusty. It's impossible that we've used all that paraffin."

Moominmamma sighed. "Now we shall have to manage with the light of the fire in the stove," she said. "There are only three candles left and I must put them on the fisherman's birthday cake." She put some more wood on the fire and left the door of the stove open.

The fire crackled cheerfully, and the family pulled the boxes in a small semi-circle round it. From time to time the storm whistled in the chimney. It was a lonely, melancholy sound.

"I wonder what's happening outside?" said Moominmamma.

"I can tell you," Moominpappa answered. "The island is going to bed. I can assure you that it is going to bed and will go to sleep at about the same time as we do."

Moominmamma laughed a little. Then she said thoughtfully: "Do you know, all the time we've been living here like this, I've had the feeling that we're on an expedition somewhere. Everything is so different all the time, as if it was Sunday every day. I'm beginning to wonder whether it's a good feeling after all."

The others waited for her to go on.

"Of course we can't always be on an expedition. It has to come to an end sometime. I'm terribly afraid that it will suddenly feel like Monday again and then I shan't be able to feel that any of this has been real . . ." She was silent and looked at Moominpappa a little hesitantly.

"But of course it's real," said Moominpappa amazed. "And it's fine to feel that it's always Sunday. It's just that feeling that we had lost."

"What *are* you talking about?" asked Little My.

Moomintroll stretched his legs. He had a feeling too, all over. He could only think of the Groke. "I think I'll go outside for a while," he said.

The others looked at him.

"I want a breath of fresh air," he said impatiently. "I can't sit here stewing any longer. I need some exercise."

"Now, listen," Moominpappa began, but Moominmamma said: "All right, go outside if you feel like it."

"What's come over him?" asked Moominpappa when Moomintroll had gone.

"It's growing pains," said Moominmamma. "He doesn't understand what's wrong with him either. You never seem to realise that he's growing up. You seem to think he's still a little boy."

"Of course he's still quite small," said Moominpappa somewhat surprised.

Moominmamma laughed and poked the fire. It was really much nicer than candlelight.

*   *   *

The Groke sat waiting on the beach. Moomintroll came towards her without the hurricane lamp. He stopped by the boat and looked at her. There was nothing he could do for her.

He could hear the beating of the island's heart, and the sound of the stones and the trees moving slowly away from the sea. There was nothing he could do to stop it.

Suddenly the Groke started to sing. Her skirts fluttered as she swayed to and fro, stamping on the sand and doing her best to show him that she was pleased to see him.

Moomintroll moved forwards in amazement. There was no doubt about it, the Groke was pleased to see him. She didn't mind about the hurricane lamp. She was delighted that he had come to meet her.

He stood quite still until she had finished her dance. Then he watched her shuffle off down the beach and disappear. He went and felt the sand where she had stood. It wasn't frozen hard at all, but felt the same as it always did. He listened carefully, but all he could hear was the breakers. It was as if the island had suddenly fallen asleep.

He went back home. The others were already in bed, and there were only a few glowing embers in the stove. He crept into bed and curled up.

"What did she say?" asked Little My.

"She was pleased," Moomintroll whispered back. "She didn't notice any difference."

*   *   *

On the fisherman's birthday the sky was just as clear and the storm was blowing just as hard.

"Wake up!" said Moominpappa. "Everything's all right again."

Moominmamma stuck her nose out from under the blankets. "I know," she said.

"No you don't!" cried Moominpappa proudly. "The island's calmed down, it's not afraid any more! The bushes have gone back to their proper places, and the trees will, too, as soon as they can. Well, what do you say to that?"

"Oh, how wonderful," said Moominmamma, sitting up. "It would have been very difficult to have a proper birthday party with lots of trees getting in the way all the time. Think of the dirt they would have brought in with them, too!" She thought for a moment and then added:

"I wonder whether they will go back to just the same places or choose new ones instead. Let me know when they make up their minds and I'll go and put seaweed round their roots."

"You're a dreary lot!" complained Little My. She was staring out of the window looking very disappointed. "Everything's going to be just the same as it always was. I was sure the island would sink, or float away or take off into the air! Nothing ever really happens round here!"

She looked reproachfully at Moomintroll. He laughed.

"Yes," he said. "It isn't everybody who can put a whole forest back where it belongs!"

"You're right!" exclaimed Moominpappa with delight. "Not everybody can do that, and without boasting about it afterwards, too!"

"I must say some people are in a cracking good mood this morning," said Little My. "It would be better if they looked after their crates of whisky!"

Moominpappa and Moomintroll ran to the window. The crate was still there on the point, but the point had moved quite a way out to sea.

"I can do without breakfast," said Moominpappa putting his hat on. "I must go down and see how high the water is."

"Have a look for the fisherman while you're about it," said Moominmamma. "It would be just as well to invite him in good time."

"Yes, do!" shouted Little My. "Imagine! He might have another engagement this evening!"

But the fisherman had disappeared. Perhaps he was hiding in the thicket, sitting inside all by himself and thinking: "It's my birthday today."

*   *   *

The cake was finished and stood waiting on the table with the candles. They had hung up branches of Mountain ash and juniper and Little My had picked a bunch of hips.

"Why are you so quiet?" she asked.

"I was thinking," answered Moomintroll. He was putting a ring of tiny pebbles round the cake.

"What do you do to get her warm?" asked Little My. "I went out during the night and the sand wasn't frozen at all."

"What do you mean?" said Moomintroll, and then blushed. "You mustn't let on."

"What sort of tell-tale do you think I am?" asked Little My. "I don't care a fig for other people's secrets. And I certainly don't broadcast them all over the place. Anyway, they all come out sooner or later. Believe you me, this island has a lot of secrets, and I know them all!" She laughed mockingly and rushed off.

Moominpappa came puffing up the stairs with a load of wood. "Mamma has no idea how to use the axe," he said. "But she can saw all right. I must make enough room round the wood-pile for us to work there together."

He flung the wood down by the stove and asked: "Do you think I could give the fisherman my old top hat? I shan't want to wear it again."

"Yes, do. You've got the one the lighthouse-keeper left behind," said Moomintroll.

Moominpappa nodded and went up the ladder to look for some paper to make a parcel. He was lifting the lid of a box when he caught sight of another verse of poetry on the wall. He hadn't seen this one before. He read the lighthouse-keeper's forlorn, spidery handwriting:

> It's the third of October,
> And nobody knows,
> Soon my birthday's quite over;
> The south-wester blows.

"But it's the third of October today," thought Moominpappa with amazement. "It was the lighthouse-keeper's birthday today, too. What a coincidence!"

He found some paper and climbed down the ladder.

The others were discussing how they could get the fisherman into the lighthouse.

"He'll never come," said Little My. "He's afraid of the lighthouse. He always makes elaborate detours to avoid going past it."

"Isn't there something that would tempt him?" suggested Moomintroll. "Something pretty, perhaps. Should we sing for him?"

"Oh, dry up!" said Little My. "That would scare him off."

Moominmamma got up and walked firmly towards the door. "There's only one way," she said. "I shall go and ask the poor creature myself in the proper old-fashioned way. Little My can go and pull him out of the thicket."

*　　　　*　　　　*

When they got there, the fisherman was sitting on the edge of the thicket with a sprig of flowering thyme in his hair. He got up and stared at them, waiting for them to say something.

"Many happy returns of the day!" said Moominmamma, curtseying.

The fisherman bowed his head with great solemnity. "You're the first person who's ever remembered my birthday," he said. "I feel very honoured."

"We're having a little party for you at home," Moominmamma went on.

"In the lighthouse?" asked the fisherman, screwing up his face. "I'm not coming there!"

"Now listen to me," said Moominmamma quietly.

'There's no need for you to look at the lighthouse at all. Just shut your eyes tight and give me your hand. My, run and put the coffee on and light the candles, please dear.''

The fisherman shut his eyes and held out his hand. Moominmamma took it and led him very carefully through the heather and up to the lighthouse-rock.

"Now you must take a big step," she said.

"Yes, I know," answered the fisherman.

When the door creaked he stopped and wouldn't go on.

"There's a cake, and we've decorated the room," said Moominmamma. "And there are presents, too."

She got him over the threshold and they started to climb the stairs. The wind moaned round the walls outside and now and then one of the windows rattled. Moominmamma could feel the fisherman's hand trembling. "There's nothing to be afraid of," she said. "It's not as bad as it sounds. We shall soon be there."

She opened the door of the room and said: "Now you can open your eyes!"

The fisherman looked cautiously round. The candles were alight although it wasn't yet twilight. The table looked very nice, with a clean white tablecloth and little green sprigs at the corners. The family stood in a line waiting for him.

The fisherman looked at the cake.

"There were only three candles left," Moominmamma said, apologetically. "How old are you, if I may ask?"

"I don't remember," the fisherman muttered. His eyes moved anxiously from one window to the other and up to the trap-door.

"Many happy returns of the day," said Moominpappa. "Pray be seated!"

But the fisherman remained standing and started to make for the door.

Suddenly Little My yelled at the top of her voice: "Sit down and behave yourself!" she shouted angrily.

The fisherman was so startled that he came up to the table and sat down. Before he knew what was happening, Moominmamma had poured out the coffee and one of the others undid the parcel with the hat in it and put it on his tangled head.

He sat very still, trying to look at the hat from underneath. He wouldn't have any coffee.

"Try a little sea-grass," suggested Little My, giving him one of her presents done up in red leaves.

"You can eat that yourself!" said the fisherman politely, and the whole family laughed. It was funny to hear him say something so apt. The party was immediately more relaxed, and they went on talking easily among themselves and left him to himself for a while. After a while he took a sip of coffee. He pulled a wry face and took eight lumps of sugar, then he swallowed the lot at one go.

Then he opened Moomintroll's present. The parcel was full of the things Moomintroll had left on the beach for the sea-horses, little bits of glass, pebbles and four copper weights. The fisherman looked at the weights for a while and said: "Huh!" Then he opened the last little parcel and took out the shell with the inscription "a present from the seaside" on it, and said: "Huh!"

"That's the best of the lot," said Moomintroll. "It was washed up on the beach."

"Was it really?" said the fisherman, looking at the bottom drawer of the desk.

He got up and went slowly to the desk. The family watched him with interest. They were very surprised that he hadn't thanked them for their presents.

It was getting dark. Only a small patch of sunlight from the setting sun shone on the apple tree on the wall. The three candles were burning steadily.

The fisherman caught sight of the bird's nest on the desk.

"That should be in the chimney," he said firmly. "It's been there for years."

"We had thought we might hang it out of the window," said Moominmamma apologetically. "But we haven't got round to doing it . . ."

The fisherman stood in front of the desk looking in the mirror. He stared at Moominpappa's hat and contemplated his own unfamiliar face. Then his eyes turned to the jigsaw puzzle. He picked up a piece and fitted it in immediately, and with short sharp movements went on putting pieces in while the family got up and came and stood behind him to see what he was doing.

He completed the puzzle. It was a picture of birds flying round a lighthouse. He turned round and looked at Moominpappa.

"Now I remember," he said. "We're both wearing the wrong hat."

He took off the hat he was wearing and offered it to Moominpappa. They exchanged hats without saying a word to each other.

The lighthouse-keeper had come back.

He buttoned up his corduroy jacket and hitched up his trousers. Then he went and picked up his cup and said: "I wonder if there's any more coffee?"

Moominmamma dashed to the stove.

They all sat down again at the table, but it was very difficult to find anything to say. The lighthouse-keeper ate his piece of cake while the family looked at him a little shyly.

"I have painted a little on one of the walls," Moominmamma remarked diffidently.

"So I see," said the lighthouse-keeper. "A landscape. It makes a change, I suppose. It's well done, too. What had you thought to paint on the other wall?"

"A map, perhaps," said Moominmamma. "A map of the island, showing all the rocks and shallows and perhaps the depth of the water as well. My husband is very good at measuring the depth of the water."

The lighthouse-keeper nodded appreciatively. Moominpappa felt very pleased but still couldn't bring himself to say anything.

Little My's bright little eyes wandered from one to the other. She looked tremendously amused and as though she was about to say something really unsuitable, but she didn't.

Two of the candles had burnt right down and run over the cake. It was dark, and the storm was still raging outside. But inside it was quiet. They had seldom had such a peaceful evening.

The thought of the Groke crossed Moomintroll's mind. But he didn't feel that he *must* think about her. He would see her later as usual, but he didn't have to. Somehow he knew that she wasn't afraid of being disappointed any longer.

At last Moominpappa said something.

"I have that crate of whisky out there on your point. Do you think the wind will drop soon?"

"When a south-westerly gale sets in it can be weeks before it blows itself out. Your crate will be quite safe, don't worry," said the lighthouse-keeper.

"I thought I might go and have a look at the weather in a little while," said Moominpappa, filling his pipe. "Do you think the boat's all right?"

"Don't worry," said the lighthouse-keeper. "There's a new moon, so the water won't rise any higher."

The third candle went out, and only the glow of the fire shone over the floor.

"I've washed your sheets," said Moominmamma, "although they were quite clean. Your bed is in it's old place."

"Thank you very much," the lighthouse-keeper said, getting up from the table. "I think I'll sleep up top tonight."

They wished each other goodnight.

"Shall we walk over to the point?" asked Moominpappa. Moomintroll nodded his head.

*   *   *

Moominpappa and Moomintroll came out on the light-house-rock. The new moon was rising in the south-east. A little crescent moon—the beginning of a new month, a darker, autumn month. They walked down towards the heather.

"Pappa," said Moomintroll. "I've got something to do on the beach. I ought to meet someone there."

"All right," said Moominpappa. "See you tomorrow. So long."

"So long," said Moomintroll.

Moominpappa walked on over the island. He wasn't thinking of the crate of whisky or of the point particularly. What did one point matter? He had several of them.

He came to the edge of the water and stood watching the breakers. There was the sea—*his* sea—going past, wave after wave, foaming recklessly, raging furiously, but, somehow, tranquil at the same time. All Moominpappa's thoughts and speculations vanished. He felt completely alive from the tips of his ears to the tip of his tail. This was a moment to live to the full.

When he turned to look at the island—*his* island—he saw a beam of light shining on the sea, moving out towards the horizon and then coming back towards the shore in long, even waves.

The lighthouse was working.

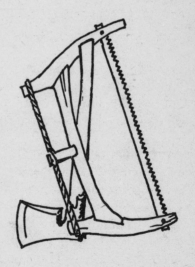